The Ghost of
ANNE
BOLEYN

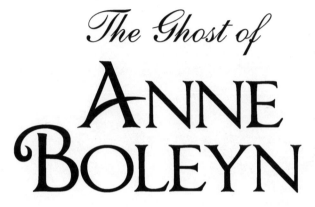

MARY DOUCETTE

authorHOUSE

AuthorHouse™
1663 Liberty Drive
Bloomington, IN 47403
www.authorhouse.com
Phone: 833-262-8899

Published by AuthorHouse 05/18/2022

ISBN: 978-1-6655-5942-3 (sc)
ISBN: 978-1-6655-5941-6 (hc)
ISBN: 978-1-6655-5940-9 (e)

Library of Congress Control Number: 2022908611

Print information available on the last page.

This book is printed on acid-free paper.

This is a work of fiction. All of the characters, names, incidents, organizations, and dialogue in this novel are either the products of the author's imagination or are used fictitiously.

To Darren,
Who would have read every draft if he could.
I hope I've made you proud.

CONTENTS

PROLOGUE

May 1536

The persistent *BANG! BANG! BANG!* of the hammer hitting the partially constructed scaffold rang like the death knell Anne knew soon awaited her. She winced each time the hammer pounded a nail for it reminded her of what it must sound like when a coffin is nailed shut. The sound was nothing more than a cruel reminder that her fate was sealed.

She couldn't stop herself from pacing. She had nothing to do but step in time with each clang and imagine parading to her own execution. It wouldn't be long now. Wringing her hands and gnawing worriedly at her lip, she let the anxiety and apprehension for the moment overtake her. She'd never have shown her worried face to the public, but in private Anne could admit to herself that she was not looking forward to dying; no one ever was, were they?

She once stood in this room on the verge of receiving her greatest desire, becoming queen. She had wanted it so badly that when Henry placed the crown on her head, it felt like she was finally receiving the offering she was due. He had sacrificed his wife, his religion, his reputation with the whole-hearted belief that Anne would bring him blessings and that was exactly what she intended to do back when she had the reward she craved: the crown and the growing baby in her belly. The one she was *sure* would be a boy and cement her future as queen like nothing else could. Anne had never known true happiness until she stood here, on the threshold of receiving everything she ever wanted.

Yet here she stood again, with her greatest happiness transforming into her greatest despair. How could so much have changed in just three short years?

She placed her hands on her flat stomach. Her barren stomach. Once full of her baby, her greatest hope, now only filled with the growing sense of nausea.

Her death loomed before her and consumed her with the same dread that gnawed at her belly every time a precious babe departed from her womb. And for nothing more than mere rumors. Rumors she was *sure* had been started by Thomas Cromwell, the filthy wretch. She wanted to spit venom just from having his name cross her mind. No one had the king's ear quite like Cromwell. She knew he hated her but could not believe he would have turned the king against her with such falsehoods. *At least be man enough to bring me down honorably,* she thought.

She would never have sunk so low as to sleep with any of the men she was accused of sleeping with. She would never debase herself so fully nor sin so horribly. She seethed at the mere implication, anger tingeing her cheeks pink. She knew she had many enemies, yet it was hard to fathom that the court was so easily swayed to believe she'd slept with her brother amongst all these men. She wondered if Cromwell's words truly held so much sway or were Katherine's supporters simply that eager to turn further against her. She knew they considered her a witch, but to cheapen her reputation as such made her think the court was morally corrupt.

While she could accept the people turning against her, the way her family had turned on her as soon as she lost the king's ear broke her heart all over again. Her uncle, the Duke of Norfolk, never craved anything so much as power, yet a small part of her hoped he would support her after she raised their family so high. He had such a strong hold on the King's opinion, and he used it to make sure she was found guilty. It was one thing for Cromwell to betray her, it was expected of her enemy, but for her own kin to turn on her because the crown mattered more to him than his own blood, that was something she'd never foreseen. Tears threatened to spill from her eyes at the thought. Her heart ached with grief and burned with vengeance.

She wasn't surprised George's wife, the lady Jane Rochford, was quick to turn against her. The woman detested George and by extension, Anne.

She had always appeared jealous of their close connection, which was nothing more than sibling love, yet the woman had claimed there was a physical component to their relationship just to see the Boleyn's fall.

And then there was Mary, her dear sister. Once they had been the very best of friends. They used to tell each other everything, whispering into the wee hours of the morning about their deepest desires and darkest fantasies. Then the king had changed all of that.

The smallest part of Anne had hoped that Mary would come to her aid while also knowing it was impossible. And why should Mary help her anyway after Anne had treated her so cruelly? Just because Mary had slept with the king long ago, and bore him a child, did not mean she held any power over him any longer. And Mary wouldn't risk putting herself in the king's path once more, not even for her own sister. She had hated the way he used her and wanted nothing more than to be rid of the affair. She never sought to use the king's attraction to her to claim the throne as Anne had. She was content to run away with her second husband, William Stafford, even though it brought her so low in the eyes of her entire family. Jealousy of Mary's pregnancy, the fact that Mary married for love, and, most importantly, the fact that Mary married without express permission from the King and Queen had led Anne and Henry to banish her from court. Anne had acted in a fit of jealousy for all her sister could obtain that was out of Anne's own reach, and the anger led to Mary's banishment. She couldn't restore their relationship now but oh, what she wouldn't give to be able to hug Mary one last time and have her tell Anne it would all be okay.

Anne tired of thinking of the family who had abandoned her. She looked down at her stomach again thinking, *I can't believe I failed. I can't believe he'd really cast me aside. I was sure he would never take me so low as execution. I was sure he'd cast me off to a nunnery like he tried with Katherine, and I would comply now, certainly I would comply. Anything was better than death. I could devote myself wholly to the Lord for the rest of my days*

Anne tossed and turned as she spent yet another night in the tower. She would die tomorrow. Less than 24 hours and she would cease to exist. It was hard to sleep when there was a nagging thought in the back of one's mind that they should stay conscious for as many hours as possible because soon, they would be eternally unconscious.

Growing up, she had never feared death. She had read the Scriptures for herself. She knew of Jesus Christ's good works and believed that good works would get her into heaven too. And she *did* do good. She might have thrown England into chaos when she won the king's heart, but she was *still* good: she gave alms to the poor, she championed commoners getting to read the Bible for themselves. All her life she thought she had been doing enough to get into heaven, but now, with the gate so close, she was doubting whether she did enough to be granted entrance. She knew she was innocent of the crimes she was accused of, so if anything would bar her entrance it would *not* be rumors made by enemies, but the what ifs plagued her since death loomed so close. And it's a lot easier to believe in good and heaven when it's a distant dream and not something with the potential to turn dastardly just lurking around the corner.

Now she was afraid. She had always held strong in her beliefs, and she tried to still, but it was so much harder when the scaffold stood just outside, ready to consume her bloody head. She wouldn't let it show to the public, but in the deepest depths of her consciousness, she was afraid. It was like the monsters from the myths had come to haunt her and there was no recourse in sight. What she wouldn't give to be a babe, swaddled in a mother's loving embrace.

She lost herself in Henry these past three years and in the need to give him a male heir above everything else but if she'd just had more time, she could have done great things for the country. She hadn't initially intended to launch a religious movement, but she would have been happy to continue leading it if Henry just gave her a second chance.

And it wasn't just fear that consumed her, but worry, not only for what would become of this movement but for what would become of her daughter. It was so easy for Henry to cast his daughter with Katherine aside and declare her a bastard. What would stop him from doing the same thing to Elizabeth? And if she were a bastard, where would she go? What fate would befall her? Anne couldn't protect her from beyond the grave, couldn't teach her how to become a strong, intelligent woman. And it caused Anne more grief than she could bear, to know that Elizabeth would have to try to survive her tyrant father and the struggles of court life without any guidance from her mother.

Her breath hitched as her lady-in-waiting, Lady Mary, tightened the laces on her crimson kirtle. She wasn't sure if she struggled to breathe from fear or because the laces were so tight.

She looked down at her hands to find them shaking once more. Always they shook. She had to breathe, had to steady herself. Anne could not fall apart on the scaffold. She came into this world destined to be a queen and, by God, she would leave this world with the dignity of one.

Her fingers lightly traced the gold B adorning her neck. She had loved that necklace once upon a time. It was a gift from Henry early in their courtship. And the B was such a prominent reminder of how high her family could climb. She might have married a Tudor, but she would never forget she started her life as a Boleyn.

Her fingers trailed up to her neck. A fair neck many had called it. Some had even written poetry about it. She wondered if this delicate thing that kept her head on her shoulders would aid her by letting her life end quickly. One quick swing of the sword and she shouldn't have to suffer long, didn't want to suffer long. In truth, she didn't want to suffer at all, but some things couldn't be avoided.

"My lady, it is time," Lady Mary said as she urged Anne's arms through her grey damask robe and slipped a mantle of ermine over her shoulders. Anne's fingers stopped shaking long enough for her to tie a white linen cap over her hair and place her gabled hood upon her head. *Good,* Anne thought, *I go to this execution with steady fingers. I once was scared, but they will not steal my calm from me.*

She unclasped her necklace and handed it to Lady Mary saying, "Keep this safe." She hoped it would end up clasped around Elizabeth's neck someday, but only God could say where her most precious ornament would end up.

At the thought of Elizabeth, Anne's eyes welled with tears. Elizabeth, her greatest joy and her greatest despair, the child that could have saved her so much heartache if she had merely been born with a different set of genitals. Could she truly have preserved Henry's love and desire for her if Elizabeth had been born male? Anne was certain the answer was a resounding yes. Anne sobbed for what could have been if she had delivered a 'Henry' rather than her dear Elizabeth nearly three years ago.

***

She could feel the splintering wood beneath her feet as she climbed the steps of the scaffold. How fitting to be pierced by wood as she would soon be pierced by cold steel. Her hands held steady as she picked up her skirts and ascended with tentative steps. She knew that for a sign of her strength. She would not cow in the face of death. She knew no guilt and for this she smiled —let the people think what they would, but she knew God would judge her innocence accordingly.

Her dark eyes pierced the crowd as she started, "I have not come to preach a sermon; I have come here to die." She continued on to ask the people to pray for the King and to pray for her, as expected in an execution speech, but she was not fool enough to expect anyone would. Half of this crowd labeled her a witch, half the crowd still prayed for their dear Katherine, and most all would believe in her guilt. For the king's word is law and he had long ago decided her fate.

She felt a sense of lightness as Lady Anne Shelton removed her hood and cloak. The cool linen draped over her eyes as Lady Mary tied her blindfold tight. With her sense of sight removed, every other sense heightened. The murmurs of the crowd sounded like poisonous words uttered straight into her ear, and the bitter taste on her tongue reminded her of just how bittersweet her love with Henry had ultimately been. The cool air felt like a lover's caress against her neck, and she couldn't help but reminisce about when Henry caressed her in the same manner. The stench of what she thought of as 'commoner London' reminded her that it didn't matter how high you climbed nor if you were once enveloped in the sweetest scents, anyone had the ability to fall so low that they died amongst the smell of shit and fish.

She wasn't subjected to the chopping block. Axes were notorious for nearly always taking several strokes to cut through, and she didn't want to suffer long. She had requested a French swordsman to ensure her death was swift. Henry had granted her request and a part of her wondered if he must still love her enough to not want to cause her any more pain than what he deemed was necessary. If it were true, he was surely showing his love in the strangest way.

Anne may not have been as devout a woman as Katherine had been, but she was still a pious woman. She kept her prayer book on her girdle, after all. In her last moments, she sought the protection and care of the Lord. Her lips formed silent prayers, words she had memorized so long ago that it took no effort to repeat them verbatim. Yet as faithful as she was, in her final minutes she couldn't stop that small vengeful part of her brain from thinking, *He will pay for what he's done.*

CHAPTER ONE

August 2019

Malorie could not believe she'd be spending another crummy, dreary day with her crummy, dreary father, but that's exactly what happened to her when the tour he planned for them of the Tower of London got postponed due to 'inclement weather'. Whatever the heck that meant. As far as Malorie was concerned, it looked like the same downpour they'd been experiencing her whole stay. London was almost always cold and gray, just like her mood.

"Mal, dear, come here for a cuppa before it gets cold," her father shouted from the other room.

She hated that nickname and had made that fact clear to him the first time he called her by it. Her name was Malorie, and *everyone* called her Malorie. She had no room in her life for cutesy nicknames. Not from friends, not from her mom, and especially not from an absent father.

See, that's what brought her to London in the first place, her absent father. Malorie had spent seven days here in London already, determined to get some answers out of the man who abandoned her and her mom fourteen years ago, when she was only two years old. Reflecting on her arrival a week ago, Malorie thought nothing had ever gone so poorly in her life. Between the initial clumsy bumping into each other that led to Malorie's suitcase toppling over and spilling her panties all over the airport floor, to Peter's attempt to placate Malorie as she shouted fourteen years' worth of angry words at him before deciding maybe getting to know him

1

first was the best approach, it was safe to say that the trip had started with a little tension.

Although her mom had remarried when Malorie was six, meaning she wasn't without a father figure for long, Malorie had never fully connected with her stepfather. Sure, he tried in little ways to kind of be a dad to her, but there was always some sort of disconnect between them. Like, no matter how many times he showed up at her softball games or made sure there was a snack waiting for her when she got home from school, she could sense the tension that poured off of him that screamed, "I didn't ask for this 'bonus' kid!!" Because of this, Malorie always longed for her *real* dad. She longed to meet the stranger whose blood she shared because she hoped he would know her and think "This is *my* kid!" She hoped he would meet her and see just how alike they were, that it would make him regret ever leaving because he missed out on getting to know his little girl, his mini-me. But at the same time, she resented him because he had the chance to know her and he threw it away. Now that she had met him, she found their personalities were at total odds with each other. Honestly, she couldn't understand what her mom saw in this man in the first place.

Her mom was a big reason she came on this trip. Now that Malorie was essentially 'coming of age' at sixteen, her mom thought it was finally time that Malorie get the answers she had yearned for her whole adolescent life.

Her dad wasn't such a dick that he never let them know where he'd run off to. They'd had his address for *years*. And he'd even sent a gift when mom got remarried. But Malorie had never been able to bring herself to write to him. She couldn't bring herself to face the truth back then. But now, at sixteen, something about the timing just felt right. So, when Malorie first expressed curiosity in reconnection, her mother had pushed for it and had even paid for the plane ticket to get her here. Fortunately, it was summer break, so she wouldn't be missing school for this reunion. Not that Malorie would have minded missing some school, but she knew her mother would not approve.

She would have been willing to travel whether it was summer break or not. She was just eager to see where this reunion got her. And, as appreciative as she should be at the fact that she was in a whole new country in a whole new time zone getting to experience a mix of cultures, she couldn't appreciate the location in its entirety. She was too keen on meeting the man responsible for her birth, curious to find out what could have taken precedence over his wife and child and why didn't he care enough about her to stay? She was also hopeful to find similarities between them, although she was loath to admit that.

When he picked her up at the airport, the similarities made themselves abundantly clear in terms of their features. They both had the same dark wavy hair, although he kept his styled in a short, professorial, dad kind-of-way and she let hers grow long and flow down her back. They both had the same too-big ears and awkwardly long hands, but what was most striking of all was the fact that their eyes were the same shade of hazel, topped with flecks of gold.

But that was where the similarities ended. On the drive from the airport to his flat, she learned he was a huge history buff. In fact, that was the field he worked in. He primarily studied the Tudor monarchy and from their first conversation, she could tell he'd spent his whole career viewing Henry VIII, whom they discussed in great detail during the ride despite the fact that she couldn't care less, like a celebrity. Meanwhile, the only celebrities she cared about were the ones she could read about in *People* magazine.

He had a great love for sports and mentioned still loving American football despite living in the UK for many years now. However, the only sport Malorie knew or cared about was Quidditch; Yeah, she was a nerd and liked Harry Potter, so sue her!

She had known there would be some tension on this trip because she was a Cancer and her weekly horoscope had said 'be wary of relationship issues, especially in regard to family,' but faux father, or 'fauxther' as she had started referring to him in her head, didn't believe in the significance of horoscopes or zodiac signs. (He was a Virgo, she soon learned, and that was honestly such a Virgo thing to say.)

Brought back to the present by the smell of cinnamon and nutmeg, Malorie had to remind herself that at least her father was making an effort. Even though he hadn't seen her for fourteen years, he learned within the past few days that the only tea she would drink was cinnamon. The Brits glared at her every time she ordered it, preferring their dull earl gray, but she didn't care. And neither, apparently, did he. At least they had this one thing in common.

At that moment, her father entered the room saying, "I made it just the way you like it, love." He handed her a saucer topped with a piping hot cup. Malorie quickly set the cup down, poured some milk in, and absentmindedly started stirring.

"Thanks, Peter," she responded. She couldn't bring herself to call him dad. Not yet. Even though he had insisted, it just didn't feel quite right. She wouldn't call him 'fauxther' to his face, she wasn't *that* disrespectful of a teenager. But 'fauxther' was who he was to her internally and 'fauxther' was who he would be in her eyes, at least for now.

A minute of silence passed before Peter attempted conversation again.

"Sorry our tour got canceled today. But luckily my manager was able to pencil us in for tomorrow. These things get booked up so fast, but we got in and I just know you're going to love it!" he said excitedly.

She wanted to believe him but so far she'd been anything but impressed. What was so impressive about a big clock and some expressionless guards with fancy, feather hats anyway?

So far, not only had nothing been entertaining, but nothing had been cheerful, which certainly didn't help with her mood. The persistent dull, gray clouds looming over her head all week reflected the same dull, gray feeling she had been feeling in her heart. She had been excited to share her overseas adventures with her boyfriend, Robbie, but he'd been so busy lately that she'd had a hard time contacting him throughout the week. When the excitement about her adventures turned to wanting to vent about all of the problems that had started cropping up or about the distance she still felt between herself and her dad and her annoyance about him trying too hard, all Robbie could give her when he *did* pick up the phone was one-word answers. It always seemed like he was only half tuned in to these conversations with her. And not only was the weather and Robbie partially at fault for her consistently gloomy mood, but so was the fact that the weather left her in a constant state of damp socks and frizzy hair!

Tomorrow's touristy activity included a tour of the Tower of London arranged by her father's company, City Wonders. And what a wonder he thought this city was. London was the whole reason he left all those years ago, she learned. He got so caught up in chasing history that he couldn't be bothered with his family anymore. At least that's what it felt like. The way he told the story was that it was a once-in-a-lifetime opportunity and he could barely afford to uproot his own life, let alone his wife and kid! As glad as she was to have that curiosity sated, she couldn't deny that the truth of the matter wounded her deeply. She was trying to be open to this reconnection with her father, but she was wary after being abandoned so long ago.

Malorie had to admit, the Tower *did* sound a little interesting. From what she could remember from middle school history classes, she was pretty sure a couple of queens had gotten beheaded there. She was also pretty sure Peter had brought that fact up with her sometime throughout the week, but it had clearly gone in one ear and out the other. She had a feeling that this tower's history was going to be a lot more entertaining than stuffy guards in silly hats or learning about wars in history class that she had zero interest in.

"It's okay, Peter. It's not like you can control the weather!" she joked. She tried to be cordial. It was the best she could do right now. And humor was her defense mechanism when she didn't know how else to handle an emotion. She knew he was making an effort and, so far, this was the best she could give him. She believed, since he saved the tour for last, that this must be his last-ditch effort to sway her, to convince her he had decent reasons for coming here all those years ago. She hoped he was right. She hoped this tower could work some magic and truly impress her.

He didn't laugh at her light-heartedness, but his eyes brightened a little. "Well, best get some rest, dear. We have a long day ahead of us tomorrow."

CHAPTER TWO

Malorie couldn't help waking up with a smile on her face. The sun was casting an orange glow on her closed eyelids so she knew she could at least wear her converse without risking water damage on her final day of touring London.

Just twenty-four more hours until this trip was done, until she could stop pretending there was any connection between her and her father and she could see her friends, maybe even plan a mall trip! Maybe even see Robbie if he was finally willing to give her the time of day. And Lord knew she could use a few new pairs of shoes after walking in nothing but puddles and mud for a week.

She took her time dressing this morning, taking care to get her bun just the right level of messy and making sure the logo of her band tee was centered just right. She *did* want to make an effort for her dad, although she wasn't entirely sure why, and he told her she could dress casual today. She wasn't one to pass up an opportunity like that. She had a feeling that despite how poorly her trip to London had gone so far that today was going to be a good day. She couldn't really explain why she felt that way. Something just pulled at her.

"Mal, love, it's time to go," her father shouted from the other room.

"It's Malorie, not Mal," she huffed. "Can't you respect what I want to be called? Can't you get my name right?" she asked angrily as she trudged into the room. She wasn't a fan of letting *anyone* shorten her name, especially not someone who hadn't taken the time to get to know what nicknames she hated.

"I'm sorry, Mal —er, Malorie. It was just a slip of the tongue. You don't need to be so rude when you speak to me." He spoke in an authoritative voice, letting her know just who was in charge in this scenario.

"Get my name right and I won't have to be so rude," she retorted, an angry gleam alight in her eyes.

"Young lady, don't you speak to me that way. You are in my care, and you will speak respectfully to me in my household!"

"Big surprise, you want to act like the dad figure now. It's a little too late for that, buddy," she mumbled under her breath.

"What was that?" he asked, detecting that she made a comment that was not so polite.

"Nothing," she answered. "Let's get going." Having said her piece, the fight had drained out of her. She just wanted to get started with the day.

But fighting with Peter now was a vivid reminder of how their first meeting at the airport a week ago had gone. If she thought there was animosity bristling between them now, it was nothing compared to the absolute rage that seeped from her pores when she first set eyes on him in Heathrow a week ago.

She had spent the whole seven-hour plane ride thinking of the things she wanted to say to him, the pent-up things that had been brewing for fourteen years. But at the same time, when they first locked eyes and she saw the same gold flecks in his that were in hers, she almost lost her resolve to fight. How could she be mad when she saw herself in front of her and when she was finally going to get the answers she so desperately craved?

She managed to perform the polite, cursory greetings towards him while they picked up her luggage in the baggage claim. She wouldn't let the anger and hurt overcome her sense of common sense and she wouldn't make a scene in public. He might deserve a tongue lashing from her, but nobody deserved the acute, judgmental stares of strangers in a public setting.

But when they were in private, driving back to his flat, she finally released every thought she had accrued over fourteen years, every angry introspection over every missed birthday, every disappointment over not seeing his smiling face in the crowds every time she won an award.

She remembered the conversation like it was yesterday. Admittedly, it's hard to forget many details when the conversation only took place a week ago. And she remembered the tenuous resolution that was reached. A resolution that sometimes had her walking on eggshells trying to contain her anger and at other times had her heart bursting with forgiveness because he might have been gone too long for her liking, but he was here *now* and every action showed he still cared about her and wanted to make it up to her.

The steady clicking of Peter's turning signal was deafening in the otherwise silent car as Peter took a right out of the airport parking lot.

"So, what's your favorite—"

"Why did you leave?" Malorie asked, cutting him off before he could even bother with whatever arbitrary question he wanted to ask. She had no time to dawdle. She was here for answers and could care less about telling Peter what her favorite color, food, band, movie, etc. was.

Peter shifted uncomfortably. A slight frown creased his face as if he was hoping they'd have more time before they dived into something this deep.

"Well, sweetheart, I—"

"DON'T call me sweetheart. You lost the right to sweet nicknames when you decided you didn't want to be my parent anymore," Malorie retorted.

"Well, Mal, it's not as simple as—"

"And DON'T call me, Mal," she interrupted once more. "You'd know I absolutely hate that nickname if you had bothered to stick around. Nobody calls me Mal. Not even mom."

"I'm sorry, swee—. I'm sorry," Peter answered earnestly. "But it's not as simple as all that. I had to leave when I did. And I didn't want to leave my family. Believe me, I cruxed over it for so long. Your mother and I debated for weeks about should or shouldn't I before I finally accepted the promotion."

"So, money mattered more to you? I was your baby girl then! Didn't you care about being in my life!?!" Malorie practically screamed.

"Of course I did! You can't say I didn't love you! You know I tried! I sent you letters. I tried to keep in contact. It was you who grew away from me," Peter yelled, anger tingeing his voice now.

He continued, "It was never just about the money. It was an opportunity I knew I'd never get again. I couldn't pass it up or I might as well say goodbye to my career."

"But *family* should have mattered more to you than some silly job. *I* should have mattered more to you," Malorie retorted, tears beginning to flow down her cheeks. She hated showing weakness like this, but she needed answers. She knew she needed to put everything on the table and there was no turning back now.

"You don't understand. You couldn't understand. My company wouldn't pay for me to relocate my family. The offer was only available to me. And I couldn't afford to house the three of us in London. I'd have gone bankrupt. So, it was either give up a once in a lifetime opportunity to stay in America with my family or move to London alone," Peter finished lamely.

"You should have stayed! Why weren't we enough for you to stay?!" Malorie practically sobbed.

Tears leaked from Peter's eyes as he said, "You have no idea the sacrifice I made all of those years ago. It killed me to leave. I loved you and your mom *so* much. I still do. I cried for weeks after I moved. It broke my heart knowing you two were a whole ocean away. But this job, I dreamed of this job since I was a little boy. I knew if I didn't pursue it, there would always be a hole in my heart. I thought I could mend the hole I'd make if I left you two. But if I didn't pursue this job, the hole would exist forever. There'd be no mending that I could do.

I tried with your mother, you know. I tried to maintain our relationship. I would take weekend trips to see her, send her gifts from London, call her every night. But it wasn't enough for her. Eventually she stopped answering the phone. And before I knew it, Marc was in her life. I didn't want to hinder her happiness, especially when I had already done so much damage. So I let her go."

"Don't you dare try to play the victim and lay all the blame on mom. I know she missed you. I know she wanted you around. And *you* broke our family apart!" Malorie was seething now, practically foaming at the lips.

"I'm not blaming your mother. I'm saying we shared equal parts in the disintegration of the relationship. And you're right. I should have tried harder with you. I should have insisted on more face-to-face meetings.

But once your mom remarried, I thought, well, she'll have an everyday dad now. A dad who can provide for her in ways I can't. What will she want with me? I wanted you to have the father-daughter relationship you deserved. And I thought you wanted it with Marc. I thought Marc would make you happy, so I stepped aside. I didn't want to get in the way of your happiness. But I couldn't resist sending you gifts and letters. I wanted you to know me. To know I'd never give up on you, even if I was letting another man be a dad to you," Peter said.

Malorie sighed and let her shoulders relax. If she truly thought about it, he *had* tried for all of these years, and *she* had been the one to pull away. She had let bitterness and resentment harbor a strong enough hold on her that she'd kept her distance from her father for all of these years. Was she really going to let resentment keep holding her back?

"I didn't want another dad. I wanted you. But I can see what you're saying. I *did* shut down on you. It was so easy to blame you. And I hadn't fully considered mom's role in all of this.

I'm sorry. I want to hate you so much. I've been hurting for so long. But maybe this thing is worth mending. Maybe we can take baby steps towards it," Malorie said, ending on a hopeful note.

"I'd like that. I'm so, so sorry too. I didn't think my actions would have caused so much damage. I thought I had tried hard enough all of these years, but I guess I should have tried harder. I should have found a way to pursue my dream without leaving my family behind. I hope you can forgive me," Peter said.

"I'm not gonna lie, I have some reservations. But I'll try to be open to mending this," Malorie said, gesturing between the two of them. "Just don't expect me to be so lovey-dovey right off the bat, okay?" she said, with a chuckle. "I need some time."

"I get it, love. Like you said, we'll take baby steps," Peter said, and with that tentative truce reached, he pulled into the driveway of his flat. Let the vacation begin.

CHAPTER THREE

─────◈─────

It felt like Malorie had aged fifty years by the time she reached the ticket stands. There must have been hundreds, if not thousands, of people here today eager to see some British history. She couldn't believe anyone could care so much. But as her father handed their tickets over to the attendant and ushered her inside, she couldn't deny she felt her jaw drop. It seemed as though there were dozens of turrets, and she could imagine a moat around the castle where the perfectly manicured lawn now stood. Malorie felt like she was looking at something straight out of *Game of Thrones*. She wouldn't have been surprised to see a queen in a nice shiny dress and tall bejeweled crown walking around, expecting her to curtsy. Or maybe a handsome knight on a big black horse, ready to swoop down and hand her a rose. It was hard to imagine that this was once a place where people were executed.

As glamorous as the 'execution castle' was, (because yes, that is what she planned on referring to it as in her head from here on out) Malorie couldn't help but be a little distracted. The day was not only sunny, it was sweltering. She was starting to regret wearing sneakers and not an open-toed shoe for this day of touristy activities. She fanned herself with the program she was handed at the entrance and telepathically willed Peter to pick up his pace and get them into a hopefully air-conditioned room!

"Our first stop is Traitors' Gate," her father said, snapping her focus back on him. "Edward I ordered this gate to be built in the 1270s in order to transport prisoners into the tower. Prisoners were brought by barge along the Thames and forced to travel past the heads of recently executed prisoners displayed on spikes. Notable prisoners that were suspected to have traveled through the Traitors' Gate include Queen Anne Boleyn, Lady Margaret Pole, and Sir Thomas More," her father stated, quite matter-of-factly. He had insisted they didn't need to pay extra for the guided tour as he knew more than any tour guide; after all, he'd spent over a decade of his life studying nothing but this history. Malorie didn't want to admit it, but she found the idea of bad guys getting their heads chopped off just as exciting as queens in pretty dresses. She supposed even the torture was like *Game of Thrones* and maybe that's why the Tower excited her so much.

"That big white stone structure in the center is the White Tower, ordered to be built by William the Conqueror in the 1070s," her father explained.

As they entered the structure and headed to the second floor, her father commented, "The white stone you'll see here was actually imported from France!" Malorie saw nothing but light-colored stones and pillars. It looked as though she was in an ancient chapel. Although she didn't care much for the religion of some people who died hundreds of years ago, she had to admit it was pretty impressive that these structures could stand the test of time and still look so beautiful.

Peter continued, saying, "This chapel was built in 1080 for St. John the Evangelist. It's actually the oldest church in London!" Anything that could be the 'est' of anything, (i.e. the biggest, the longest, the oldest, the tallest) was pretty cool in her eyes.

The rounded arches and huge stone pillars combined with the way the room curved made her feel like some noble lord should magically appear and pull a fancy sword out of nowhere. Maybe she had been reading too much fantasy lately, but this truly looked like a picture one of her favorite authors might paint for her with their words.

Peter interrupted her moment of staring in wonder to say, "Under the stairs that lead to the chapel, two skeletons were found which many believe belonged to the two young boys allegedly murdered by Richard III."

At Malorie's wide-eyed stare, Peter knew he would need to provide a little more explanation, so he continued, "While Edward IV was king, he had two sons named Edward V and Richard, Duke of York. They came before their uncle, Richard of Gloucester, in the line of succession. It is speculated that in an attempt for Richard of Gloucester to win the throne, he had his young nephews kidnapped and killed in the Tower. He was

King Richard III for a short time before Henry VII defeated him in battle and took his place."

The story sounded like something straight out of a medieval soap opera. Malorie's eyes stayed voluminous and glossy as she looked around. She beamed widely for the first time this week as she thought about the danger and excitement of someone murdering their own kin for power. If she were in a movie theater, she'd be on the edge of her seat!

As her father continued the tour, Malorie felt like she'd been shown a thousand towers: Cradle tower, the Wakefield tower, the Bloody tower, the Salt tower. It felt like a thousand names were thrown at her all at once and it didn't hold her attention for very long. Her father droned on and on, and she had a hard time caring about what exactly put all of these noble people in prison.

As they entered the Martin tower, something in the stone caught Malorie's attention. She read BOULLEN etched into the stone and chuckled to herself. "Hehe, 'boullen' sounds like 'bouillon', like a bouillon cube. Who was thinking about making soup on their way to the tower?" she muttered. Once the thought escaped her lips, she found it so funny to imagine some 1500s prisoner thinking about soup that she burst out laughing. This caused some angry stares aimed her way and it was also loud enough to draw Peter's attention. He had continued walking and prattling on about history, so he hadn't initially regarded this strange etching that made Malorie stop and think.

"Ah, you noticed the 'boullen' etching," Peter remarked as he came to join her. He had a smile on his face as though this were the most precious secret the castle held.

Malorie, who had yet to successfully read the room (or yard as the case may be), hadn't noticed the serious look on her father's and the rest of the crowds' faces.

"Yeah, bouillon, like soup. Who was thinking about soup while they were imprisoned?" she asked and burst into laughter again.

"Mal, it doesn't say 'bouillon', it says 'boullen'. Like the queen. Anne Boleyn. This was an alternate spelling of the name. Although this carving was believed to be made by Anne's brother, George, as it was suspected he was imprisoned here shortly before he was executed for the rumor that he had an incestuous relationship with his sister, Anne."

Malorie couldn't believe her ears. She could hardly remember what she had learned about Anne Boleyn in school. The only thing she remembered was that she had been executed. She wasn't even entirely sure what her crime was. She was moderately curious to learn more about her since it wasn't every day that a queen slept with her brother, unless she was on *Game of Thrones* of course. Although she had to admit, she was hesitant to learn much more about this queen because she was skeptical that any new information would really hold her attention.

They entered Martin Tower and Malorie was subjected to another long lecture about all of the Crown Jewels housed here and why Peter thought they were so important.

They next stopped at the monument just outside of the Beauchamp tower. Malorie saw an odd-looking blue table that appeared to be made out of glass and couldn't help rushing over to it. When her father caught up to her, he explained, "This is a monument for the prisoners who have been executed in the tower. It was widely rumored that this monument was erected where the scaffold was once placed. Of course, I know the truth. If you ask any *true* historian, they'll tell you that the scaffold was on the north side of the White Tower." He let out a little chuckle as he said this. Malorie could hardly focus. She found her hands instinctively reaching out to touch the place where Queen Anne Boleyn's name was written in black ink. The blue table may have held hundreds of names, but Malorie's eyes were drawn to Anne's name, and only Anne's. She didn't know what possessed her to reach out and trace the smooth curve of the B in her name. There was a magnetic pull she couldn't resist and before she knew it, the soft pad of her finger was connecting with the black ink and an electric jolt coursed through her at the touch. It felt like the way a person's lips tingle after a magical first kiss. She pulled away, a little dazed and, seconds later, Peter was placing an arm gently around her shoulder and guiding her onward.

Her father next took her to what once were the royal apartments. The remains now looked mostly like crumbling stone, but she could almost imagine them in their splendor when Queen Anne lived in them, waiting for her life to end. She was amazed when they entered to find the Great Hall with its tall ceilings, stained glass windows, and large pillars. It looked so spacious. Like it could hold hundreds of jewels and tons of furniture. Her father mentioned Anne's apartments could have looked similar to this and Malorie was amazed!

Peering through the large window with its archaic, arched frame, Malorie couldn't help but wonder what it must have been like to stare out this very same glass so many centuries ago knowing you were mere hours away from being executed. Would the thought of execution make someone think about all of the good and bad they'd done in their lives? Would they wonder if they truly deserved this? She knew those were the questions that would run through her head if she were in that position.

"I need to visit the loo, love," her father called, pulling her out of her musings, before stalking off in the opposite direction. She wasn't sure how long he would be gone, and she never had the patience to just sit still so she thought *what harm could a little wandering do?* before she ventured off.

She wasn't sure where her feet were carrying her. She had lost track of all thought of time when suddenly she bumped into a wall that felt different from all of the other stones around her. Where the rest of the wall felt relatively smooth, like it had been maintained throughout the years, this section felt rough and ancient, as if it hadn't been touched since the last execution took place hundreds of years ago. She wondered how no employee had noticed this distinction. Or was she merely going insane and no ancient wall truly existed? Since these ruminations were plaguing her, she pressed just a little on the ancient stone and it felt like the wall might give! She pressed a little harder and suddenly found this small segment of wall moving forward. It shifted just a few inches forward and wouldn't budge. She soon learned she had to slide it to the left, and suddenly she was standing in front of a very narrow opening. Did she just stumble upon some sort of secret entrance?

It was so narrow she could barely shimmy her hips through. She was not the skinniest girl, and she *did* have some curves. The tight fit made her think she was not supposed to be here, but curiosity got the better of her and there was no way she was turning back now! She kept expecting to see some sort of "employees only" sign to let her know she was definitely not where she was supposed to be, but none crossed her path. She walked a few feet before she found herself at the base of what appeared to be the most old, rickety looking staircase she had ever seen. She thought *no turning back now* and started her ascent.

She had to have been climbing for ten minutes straight. Her legs were cramping, she could barely breathe, and sweat was beading on her forehead, but she found herself more determined than ever to figure out the mystery that wall was trying to hide. She worried her dad must be out of the bathroom by now and would be frantically searching for her. Maybe she should call him? She pulled out her phone to find no cell reception. *Well crap,* she thought. *But I can't give up now. I have to find out what's on the other side of this thing. I'm sure he'll be alright.*

Just a few seconds later, she found the staircase had *finally* come to an end and she was facing a large hallway with wooden floors. She hadn't noticed the lit sconces on the walls as she climbed the stairs, but now that they were gone, she could see just how dim this corridor was. It looked like she was entering something straight out of a horror film, but she couldn't stop herself from continuing to investigate. She turned her phone's flashlight on and stepped forward.

There were two large wooden doors with large brass knobs on either side of the hallway. She wasn't sure what pulled her, but she just knew she had to enter the room on the right.

Malorie reached for the dusty, brass doorknob, heart hammering so loudly she feared she'd wake the dead. The knob was cold to the touch and sent a shock through her system. The door creaked like it hadn't been oiled in millennia, but all Malorie could think about was how it sounded just like the doors from horror movies that had killers and monsters lurking on the other side. She feared that the loud squeak of the door must be alerting the hidden demons to her presence.

She let out a sigh of relief when she opened the door to reveal nothing more than a large, ornate four-poster bed on the other side. A handful of delicate chairs and a rickety table completed the room.

Dust coated every inch of the room, from the red, silk curtains hanging from the intricately carved wooden bed posts to the rich, oakwood walls to the padlock and key lying discarded on the floor, covered in their own mound of dust. *Padlock and key?* she thought. *What could these be doing here?* Either someone or something was not meant to enter or someone or something was not meant to exit. Was this a prison or a sanctuary? She shuddered and let out a nervous breath because she didn't have enough clues to answer one way or the other.

As if operating on autopilot, Malorie walked towards the bed, compelled to touch the mattress and determine if it really felt as uncomfortable as it looked. (Even from a distance, she could tell that it was not like the brand new Tempur-Pedic that she was used to back home.)

Before she could extend her hand, she saw the curtains sway with no breeze to move them and a sudden, bone-chilling cold seeped into her pores. The cold mixed with this sudden movement caused Malorie to gasp with fright. She turned to run and as she pivoted, she managed to trip over herself and landed, palms out, on the hard stone floor. Her phone skidded from her hand, flashlight still illuminating the dust and dirt in the room. The movement caused the layers of dust to swirl in the air and Malorie found herself coughing profusely.

By the time she finished hacking up a lung, she was able to look up and noticed dark patches of wood in the shape of large squares and rectangles. It looked like portraits or other wall adornments once hung here. Malorie wondered why they were taken down. *Who did this room belong to anyway?*

The chill that raked Malorie's body passed as swiftly as it had come, and she quickly found herself regaining her composure as she stood and wiped her dusty hands on her jeans. The dust left a large, gray smudge and Malorie winced as she realized not only would she have to wash these now, but she'd likely have to find some excuse to explain the mark to Peter.

As she walked over to pick up her phone, she noticed a source of light she hadn't noticed before. Weak sunlight filtered through the small window and the intersecting lines on the window left funny shadows where her phone once sat.

She glanced out the window and was fairly sure she was looking at where her father told her the gardens used to be.

I don't remember the building being this tall, she thought as her gaze lingered out the window. She felt she was higher up than she should be and the thought made her breath hitch. *Something's not right here. This place isn't normal.*

Her head was spinning, and she found herself gasping for air. *Why can't I breathe? Where am I? What is this place?* Her mind raced and she sat on the end of the bed to try to calm herself.

Breathe… in…1…2…3…. Out…1…2…3

She repeated this several times until she was able to unclench the death grip she had on the bed; her knuckles went from white to a healthy shade of rose. Once she was able to calm down, she began to look around again and noticed one panel of wood that was oddly discolored in a way that differed from where the lost paintings used to hang

That's weird, she thought. She walked over to it. An eerie calm overcame her that matched the calm and quiet that permeated the room. Although just moments ago, Malorie was undergoing a full-on panic attack, at least she's pretty sure that's what it was based on what she'd seen on TV, now she felt she'd found her purpose, as if every little moment in her entire existence had led her to touch this wall. Upon doing so, she found the wood was soft and caved in just from the poke of her fingers. *Was old wood known to crumble or was this wall just really odd?* she wondered. She firmly pushed on the wood, causing it to cave in and expose a small hole. She could see nothing but darkness but figured maybe she should feel around. She'd seen enough movies like *National Treasure* to know that something supercool usually lurked behind secret cubbyholes like this.

As she continued to dig and widen the hole with her fingers, she felt something smooth and slippery brush against her fingertips. She wasn't sure why, but the feeling reminded her of her grandma's pearls. She pulled the object out and, sure enough, she was holding a pearl necklace! From the pearls hung a golden B and, below that, were three tear-drop pearls suspended from the B.

It looked old fashioned to Malorie but, she had to admit, there was something transcendent about the jewelry.

The pearls looked like they had yellowed. She guessed they did that with age? She had never heard of such a thing before. She had to admit the necklace was beautiful and the jewels looked real. But she couldn't wrap her head around why it was here. Heck, she couldn't wrap her head around where she was, so what was one more confusion?

It was at that moment that she realized the chill was back and dread filled the pit in her stomach. Bile threatened to crawl up her throat as the cold intensified. The skin on her neck tingled and goosebumps lined her arms. Suddenly, the strands of hair that had fallen loose from her bun blew back off of her face and she was enveloped in the iciest chill she had ever experienced. The cold was so intense, it felt painful to her hands. And her teeth chattered so hard she was sure one or more of them were bound to crack.

Finally, she heard from across the room. Who was speaking in that formal British accent? She looked over to find a relatively short woman, maybe 5'2" or 5'3", standing there in a dark gown with a square neckline adorned with jewels. She wore a weird, rounded hat thing to cover most of her dark hair.

She wasn't pretty in a modern sense, but she was far from hideous. She had a long straight nose and small pursed lips, but what really caught Malorie's attention were her eyes. She had never seen eyes so large and dark. She looked like she could give you either the kindest or most piercing expression depending on how you talked to her.

"Who are you? And how did you get in here?" Malorie asked. As far as she could tell it was nearly impossible to get to this room, so she wasn't entirely sure how this woman had followed her or why she was dressed this way.

The woman looked at her with the most curious expression in her intense, dark eyes. *Who art thee? Where art mine own maids?* she asked, pausing to look all around the opulent room as if she expected her maids to come bustling forth. Malorie couldn't figure out why the woman seemed almost translucent in the dim light nor why her voice sounded muffled, almost like she was trying to speak through very thick glass. She also couldn't wrap her head around why this woman would be speaking some sort of Shakespearean English. All she knew was that this strange woman was really starting to freak her out.

"I think the actors are supposed to wait downstairs. Are you lost?" Malorie's father had told her that every few hours or so there were reenactments of some of the executions that had occurred at the Tower of London, so she could only assume that this woman was one of the performers who had simply lost her way.

I am not lost. I bethink I know mine own apartments when I see them, the strange woman answered. *Why art thee dressed in such peculiar clothing?* she continued.

Malorie was astounded that the woman should ask that question considering the state of her *own* appearance. Nevertheless, she persisted. "I think we got off on the wrong foot. My name is Malorie. Who are you?" As she asked the question, she stepped over to the woman and extended her hand for a shake. The woman hadn't acted hostile so far, so Malorie felt safe to let her guard down. She was starting to think perhaps this woman was not a performer but someone who was just really into cosplaying as queens and had somehow managed to get just as lost as she was?

When she extended her hand, she realized she still had the necklace clutched in her palm, which was growing sweatier by the minute as she dealt with this altercation. This woman must have noticed them too because she quickly exclaimed, ***Mine own jewels!***

"Listen, lady," Malorie continued. "You're really starting to freak me out. These can't be your jewels. They've gotta be hundreds of years old. And why are you acting like you're not from this century anyway? Quit the act, tell me who you are, and we can figure out a way to get out of here."

You dare speak to me so rudely? I am a queen, those art mine own jewels, and I am not going anywhere. I have been sent here to die, so die I must, as the King commands it. Upon the morrow, mine own ladies shall take me to the scaffold, the woman answered defiantly, a fierce gleam entering her eyes.

Malorie started to piece together everything she knew from history class and everything her father had been telling her the past few days. A queen with a B necklace awaiting execution? This lady couldn't seriously think she was Anne Boleyn, could she?

"Hey lady, are you seriously trying to tell me you're Anne Boleyn?" Malorie asked.

Of course, I am Anne Boleyn, the woman (Malorie refused to think of this lady as the *real* Anne Boleyn) answered.

Malorie said, more to herself than the woman, "This is absolutely impossible. It's the 21st century! You've been dead for like 500 years! This can't be real. I must have knocked myself out and fallen down some stairs. This must all be a dream." Malorie paced as she spoke out loud, her eyes flitting all over the room, trying to make sense of the experience unfolding before her. Her mumbling intensified and she started pacing more frantically. She had completely tuned out this woman just trying to convince herself that she wasn't going insane.

That is not your property! "Anne" screeched, ignoring Malorie's frantic stammering. Either she had no idea what Malorie had said or she was so singularly focused on the necklace that the words hadn't registered. Either way, she seemed ready to treat Malorie like a bug she was prepared to squash unless she got her necklace back. The cruel intensity radiating off of her translucent body was almost palpable.

"Anne's" anger bristled off of her opaque skin and Malorie knew if she could be steaming right now, she would be. Her hands, clenched into fists at her side, shook as she said, *Give me what is mine or be prepared to face the consequences.*

Her voice had become low and deadly. Her lip curled in disgust like Malorie was a despicable creature who couldn't do anything but be in the way.

Her stare burned molten hot and before the movement registered in Malorie's brain, "Anne Boleyn" lunged toward her in an attempt to take the necklace. As her dainty, porcelain white hand crashed into Malorie's, it was like watching flesh dissipate into a puff of mist. Malorie suddenly felt colder than she'd ever felt before, like she had just dumped her hand in a bucket of ice. Despite the intense pain that the sudden cold caused her, Malorie was frozen in place and found her grip tightening on the necklace rather than relaxing. She clutched the necklace so tightly she felt the B leaving an indent in her palm, yet still she couldn't let go. All she could manage to do was look at this woman in wide-eyed horror. She didn't care if this woman was crazy, she didn't care if this woman was lost, all she knew was that she had to get the hell out of here.

The woman howled with rage before lunging once more. Malorie recovered long enough to sidestep her, turn, and bolt for the exit. As she ran, she managed to toss the necklace into her jacket pocket, the one she had tied around her waist after realizing just how hot the day turned out to be. Her hands were slick with sweat, so she fumbled with the door. She was terrified of those pale arms, fearing she'd be grabbed again and plunged into a glacial prison with no escape. But not even the sound of her feet thundering down the stairs could drown out the tormented howl that echoed down the hallway, as if the nightmare would continue to chase her.

CHAPTER FOUR

Malorie fled as fast as she could, taking the stairs two at a time. She didn't care that they were steep and crooked and that she could probably break her neck flying down them at this speed, all she knew was that she had to get away from the crazy lady who turned to mist and who thought she was Anne Boleyn.

None of this was possible. She had to find a way to rationalize things; that's what she did, that's what she always did when she was scared or overwhelmed.

Okay, she thought as she ran faster than she had ever run in her life (sports were never really her thing, after all). *It was just some crazy lady. She must have been dressed weirdly and speaking strangely because she was into medieval cosplay, or she was one of the paid actors. And there's nothing strange about that! The room was cold because it wasn't insulated. Her hand didn't turn to mist, that was just a trick of the light.*

Yes, yes! It all made sense! Of course it did! She had nothing to fear and absolutely nothing to tell her dad. She just got lost. She could tell him that much. She didn't need to worry him with the details. She hoped he hadn't called UK police for her or something. She just wanted to get out of here now with as little fuss as possible. She wanted more than anything to go home. And not her dad's home either. She wanted to be back in America and in her mother's arms. If she never heard another British accent again, well, that would just be the best thing in her life.

This place was strange, the people were strange, and she didn't want to take another second of this. She couldn't believe she actually thought today would be a good day. But all she got was another bad day tacked onto an already miserable week.

All week, Malorie felt lonely. Conversations with her dad were filled with tension and she could barely speak to her mom or friends because phone calls overseas were so expensive. When she *did* try to call home on days she thought she could spare the expense, it was her boyfriend, Robbie who she tried to call. And it didn't help that she was lucky if Robbie even bothered to pick up the phone. All she wanted was a friend to gripe with about the bad weather and the boring activities. She felt so out of place amongst all of these people who looked and sounded so different from her. Her dad was still a stranger to her, and she was having trouble bridging the gap there. All she'd wanted all week was the comfort of her best friend to make her feel a little less like an outsider. If fate had decided to answer her prayers for companionship by sending this weird ghost lady her way, well, she was ready to raise her fists and curse the sky for this very not funny joke.

She found her way back to Winchester Hall to find her dad surrounded by men in black vests and funny hats. It looked like a couple of them were holding walkie-talkies, and she prayed to God that they weren't calling for backup.

Okay, we need to think of some excuse for why we were gone that won't get us sent to the police station or the looney bin, she thought. She looked down at her pants and noticed the dust smudges. She tried to brush them off to no avail. *Please, God, let him think this is fashionable and my pants just look like this! Please don't let him question where the dirt came from!*

At that moment, her father locked eyes with her. "Mal, love, where have you been?" he asked with a hint of panic in his voice. "You've been gone for 45 minutes! I was worried sick! I had to call in the Bobbies!" he said in such a rush, she had a hard time dissecting his words. His accent got stronger under strong emotion, so she practically needed a translator to understand him.

"Peter. I'm okay. Really. You can calm down now. I swear I'm okay. I just went to check out the gift shop and lost track of time." *Yes, that would do for a decent lie,* she thought.

"I checked the gift shop, love. I didn't see you anywhere," her father said, his voice managing to sound even more frantic. And did she detect a hint of annoyance? As if his dad-sensors were going off on overdrive and he knew dang well she was lying to him.

Crap. So much for that lie, Malorie mused to herself. "Um, well, you must have just missed me then because that's where I definitely was. 100 percent," Malorie said. The lie sounded weak even to her own ears and she really hoped her father didn't question her any further. If he did, she was absolutely a goner because she was sure there were security cameras in the gift shop. Her lie could easily be unraveled in mere seconds, so she muttered to herself, *Please believe me. Please believe me. Please believe me!*

"Well, fine. But don't ever do that to me again," her father continued. "I don't know what I would have done if I'd lost you for good. I'd be beside myself."

Yeah, nice of you to finally care now, she thought, contempt lacing her inner thoughts. But she kept that to herself. She was more relieved to not be caught, and there was no sense adding negativity to an already high-strung moment.

"I'm sorry, Peter. I really am. But this has been pretty intense. Can we just head home now?" she asked, weariness lacing her voice. She still had dark eyes and misty hands running through her mind and wanted to get away from these ancient structures as soon as possible.

"Of course, love. We'll head straight home and have a cuppa to calm our nerves," he answered, placing an arm around her gently. She had previously made it known that she did not care for physical contact from him, but she felt now was not the time to remind him, and anyways, the firm yet soft pressure of his fingers as he gave her shoulder a squeeze *was* quite comforting in this moment.

She couldn't believe just how frayed her nerves were from that strange cosplay/actress lady. *Never mind it,* she thought. *I just need to get through this night and I'll be back in America in no time. Then I'll get to leave crazy British ladies behind me once and for all.*

"Mal, are you sure you're all right?" her father asked as he cradled his cup of tea in his large, callused hands. "You're looking a little peaky, love," he continued.

He was leaning back in his favorite recliner, the leather so cracked it was more white than red now and the cushion so worn that he sunk into it a good five inches. But he loved it and it *did* make the room cozy. Malorie knew all he wanted was to make this place warm and inviting for her, and she had to admit she was starting to lower her defenses and just let him.

It scared her to think of lowering her walls for this man. He left fourteen years ago of his own volition and Malorie couldn't rationalize why he'd deserve to know her and be kind to her *now!* Like, he had his chance, and he blew it. End of story, right? But he *was* trying, and a part of Malorie thought it was just too much effort to hold a grudge when so much effort was being put into caring about her happiness and wellbeing. It took more than just a week to win back someone's love when you'd been gone for fourteen years so she knew she'd be wrestling with these feelings for a while.

As he asked after her health, he attempted to exit his chair in order to place a hand on her forehead to check her temperature. It took a few grunts from Peter and a few squeaks from the chair before he finally managed to cross the room and place his rough, calloused fingers against her forehead.

His brows knit in concern as he said, "You're feeling a little warm, love." She could tell by his face that he was worried about her, and she could tell by his tone of voice that he was trying to remain casual and not baby her. He must have known by now that babying is the *last* thing she'd ever want from him.

"Dad, please. I'm fine," she said, perhaps a little too roughly, as she brushed his fingers away from her face. She noticed too, that she'd only really been calling him dad lately, not just Peter anymore. When had that happened? And why had it happened? Did that crazy British lady really scare her so much that she needed comfort from her dad? Perhaps, but she wasn't ready to admit that just yet. She wasn't ready to admit that lady was anything other than a seriously weird hallucination she must have gotten after tripping and hurting herself. Half of those towers had stairs that were practically death traps after all. It was a small wonder that there weren't *more* tourists who came through complaining of bruises and concussions.

"Well, you really *do* look pale, love. And you're feeling a little clammy. Maybe you should go to bed a little early and get some rest. You have a big day tomorrow and a long, tiring journey ahead of you," her dad exclaimed with a gleam in his eye. She supposed that meant he was back to his old self, ready to trust she was okay and not worry about her so much.

"You're right, Peter. I think I'll head to my room now and get some rest." She felt a sense of ease at calling him by his name again. "Dad" only slipped out because she was scared and confused but she wouldn't let herself be overwhelmed by weakness any longer! Just because he'd acted caring this past week did not mean she'd revert to thinking of him as "dad." He'd been out of her life way too long thus far to deserve that. Right?

Malorie entered the room her dad had fixed up for her for the week. It was clear he was the type of father who made an effort but didn't know a thing about what she was really into as the walls were plastered with boy bands she hadn't heard of, stuffed animals and pony figurines she had long ago outgrown, and a hot pink comforter that was *so* far from her favorite color. She wanted to roll her eyes and make some snide comment like, 'Of course he didn't know what she liked. He didn't take the time to get to know her all these years!' But when she really thought about it, she figured this would be a move any dad would make. Dads always seemed to be pretty oblivious about what trends their kids were really into. She laughed to herself at that thought.

She sat on her bed and pulled out her phone. The clock read 9:01pm. *Great, that means it's about 4 o' clock back home. Robbie's class should have just ended. Maybe I'll give him a call.*

As she listened to the dial tone, she contemplated what exactly she'd tell Robbie about her day. She obviously couldn't tell him she saw a ghost but maybe she'd tell him that the tour they went on wasn't so bad after all.

After the sixth ring, he finally picked up and her heart raced.

"Hullo?" a gruff voice answered on the other end.

"Hey, Robbie, it's me! How are you, sweetie?" Malorie asked excitedly.

"Fine," Robbie answered.

Malorie paused, hoping he'd add more to the conversation. When he didn't, she continued, "So, guess what! Peter wasn't as much of a boring, old nerd today." She chuckled at her own comment before adding, "And I had a lot of fun at the Tower of London! There were a lot of cool looking structures and I learned about a bunch of executions that took place there!"

Malorie paused for breath, cruxing over what else she could divulge. But before she got a chance to start speaking again, Robbie said, "That's nice, babe. Listen, I gotta go. I got a lot of, uhhhh, homework." He paused for a long moment between the last two words, making it seem like he was reaching for the word "homework" as his excuse.

Still, Malorie persisted. "But, it's only been–"

She heard the click on his end of the line before she could even finish the sentence. "– a few minutes," she finished lamely, muttering in defeat.

She couldn't fathom why he was being so distant. Nothing had changed between them except this college summer program he was in now. She decided right then and there that this had gone on long enough and she was going to have a serious conversation with him when she got home. They needed to iron this out.

As she sat on her bed, reliving the day's events, she felt the weight of the necklace still in her pocket. This prompted her to unlock her phone once more and do a quick Google search of Anne Boleyn. Over and over again she saw the dark hooded eyes she had seen in that ancient room staring back at her. What scared her even more was that in nearly every portrait she was wearing the same dark dress and dark, round head covering. The woman in this portrait could easily be the twin of the woman she had seen in that dusty, old room. This was uncanny.

She finally tore her gaze away from those intense eyes to notice the B necklace encircling her neck. Malorie felt like she'd just been punched in the gut. Her mouth hung open, but no air could pass through her lips.

No. It couldn't be. That couldn't be the necklace currently sitting in her pocket. Could it? She clicked on dozens of photos of the same woman in the same dark dress with the same B necklace around her neck, enlarging the photos whenever she could so she could study the necklace intensely. She was scared to notice that the pearls in every single photo had the same shape as the pearls in her pocket.

She reached down to touch the bulge in her pocket. It felt like a white-hot iron was blazing in her pocket. She was terrified and wanted to fling the necklace as far away from her as she could. But she was also scared to touch it again, remembering what had happened the last time.

Okay, I need to rationalize this, she thought. There was sense to be made out of this situation and, by God, she would find it. *The necklace currently residing in my pocket is probably just some cheap gift shop knockoff necklace. Yes! That makes sense. We were in the Tower of London, the place Anne Boleyn died. It would make sense for the gift shop to carry her necklace as a souvenir. After all, I hadn't actually entered the gift shop even though I told Peter I had, so perhaps there actually were novelty Anne Boleyn necklaces in the store!* And what was she so afraid of anyway? So, she found a cheap necklace that someone must have bought at the gift shop and then accidentally dropped. So what? There was no way this tiny thing held all this power. She was just building it up in her mind.

She closed her eyes and pulled out the necklace. Her fingertips caressed the smooth, cool pearls before lightly tracing the golden B. She could feel every intricacy in the necklace and was terrified her clammy hands would somehow damage the material.

She squeezed her eyes shut even tighter and felt her breath hitch as that cold burst of air she had felt mere hours ago reappeared. She was scared to open her eyes, which was absurd because the blast must have been from the air conditioner her dad had made sure to install in her room before she arrived.

Nothing supernatural is going on here, she told herself before opening her eyes.

Dark eyes were mere inches from her face, glistening with anger. It took all of Malorie's energy not to let out a blood curdling scream (she didn't want to alert her dad to the trouble after all). As it was, she ended up biting down on her hand so hard she tasted blood just to keep herself from screaming.

Sweat dampened her skin and the rattle of pearls reminded her that the jewels were still clutched in her now trembling hand.

"How… How… How are you here?" she choked out the sentence. It took all of her energy just to talk. She was so scared that she could hardly form words. She had lost all sense of rationalizing events when this woman materialized in front of her. It was time to face the facts that, as impossible as it seemed, Malorie was facing a ghost right now.

Giveth me mine own necklace, the woman shrieked. She was no longer the proud looking woman with the haughty air to her. She was manic. The way tendrils of hair blew around her face and her hand stretched out like a claw made her look ethereal, and not in a good way. She reminded Malorie of that scene from *The Little Mermaid* when Vanessa gets all crazed right before she turns back into Ursula.

"Just leave me alone!" Malorie cried, flinging the necklace against her pillow, (even amongst the intense emotions she was feeling, she couldn't bring herself to damage the precious jewels). She collapsed on the bed and buried her head in her arms and in that moment, she noticed that the temperature had returned to normal. The woman wasn't speaking to her anymore. In fact, the silence was so intense that it took on an eerie quality.

Malorie looked up to realize the woman was gone. *That's strange. Why would the ghost lady disappear when I clearly never gave her what she wanted? And how did she follow me here in the first place?*

As Malorie tried to puzzle out this bizarre apparition, her eye caught the glint of the gold B on the necklace she had just thrown. Could the lady be connected to the necklace? She knew the only way to test it was to see if touching the necklace made her reappear, but she was terrified. This was one experiment she was so far from willing to perform. Still, if she did nothing, if she just left the necklace alone, her dad might stumble upon it and become the haunted one. Even if she took efforts to throw the necklace away, she was afraid it might behave like those cursed objects in movies that just keep reappearing. She was sure if she didn't solve the mystery of this cursed necklace, that this woman—let's face it, the ghost of Anne Boleyn—would find someone new to haunt. She was afraid the horror would always be present unless she did something about it right now.

But should she summon this ghost? Would it *really* be so bad if she just left well enough alone? A part of her wanted to address it now so it didn't end up biting Peter in the butt somewhere down the road. She may have mixed feelings about the man, but not even her worst enemy deserved to be haunted. And she was scared and that was the biggest reason she wanted to never touch this necklace again. Yet every time she touched it, she felt alive and nothing else had ever made her feel this way before. She loved solving mysteries as a girl, and she itched to crack this case wide open.

Taking tentative steps toward her pillow, she gently reached a finger out. This was the moment of truth, no backing out now. She knew if the ghost of Anne Boleyn appeared as soon as she touched this necklace, then she should solve the mystery that would put this spirit to rest once and for all. After all, that's how it worked in the TV shows, right?

The pad of her index finger lightly grazed just one tiny pearl and Anne immediately materialized in a swirl of mist. Instead of yelling at her, as seemed to be Anne's custom, she immediately lunged for the necklace once more. Her hands sank right through the fuzzy, pink pillow and, if Malorie hadn't been looking, she would have missed the look of complete bafflement that crossed her face.

Where am I? Anne asked, a note of desperation in her voice. She peered around frantically, and Malorie realized that Anne had been so intent on the necklace this whole time that she hadn't taken in her surroundings.

This was the first time she didn't sound in control of herself. She sounded as scared as Malorie had been feeling from the moment Anne entered her life. Malorie decided since Anne was finally not shouting at her or trying to attack her that she could try to answer her as civilly as possible. After all, if she didn't at least attempt to question the woman, she was never going to solve this mystery.

"Um, you're in my bedroom. In my dad's apartment. Well, they call it a flat here. We're on, well, I don't remember the name of the street actually. But you can see Big Ben from the window. And that giant Ferris wheel on the other side." She pointed to each attraction as she spoke.

Malorie realized that she was babbling, and that this apparition probably had no idea what she was saying, especially if she was from the 16th century as she claimed. Malorie probably sounded like she was speaking a foreign language to Anne's ears.

"I'm sorry. You probably have no idea what I'm saying right now."

Mine own maids. Mine own furnishings. Where is't all? Anne interrupted, a frantic note in her voice.

Anne circled the room, madly attempting to sweep her hands across the walls, dresser, anything she could attempt to get her permeable hands on. It was at this point that Malorie realized Anne wasn't just struggling with being in the 21st century, Malorie was pretty sure her spirit had never left the Tower of London before!

Where am I? Anne asked again, panic lacing her tone, her voice tinged with desperation.

Malorie figured if she was going to solve this mystery, she had to start with some simple questions she was sure Anne could answer for her. "Have you truly never left the Tower of London since you died?" Malorie asked.

I'm dead? Anne shrieked, translucent tears staining her pearly cheeks.

Well, maybe that wasn't the best way to start it, Malorie! She couldn't believe the woman who came across so haughty and regal when they first met could so totally lose her composure. But she supposed she would be in the same boat if she had just found out she was dead. Wait until Malorie told her she'd been dead for almost 500 years!

In the gentlest voice Malorie could muster, she wanted to get the truth through to Anne as soon as possible so they could proceed with solving the mystery, she said, "Okay, um, there's a lot to explain to you right now. Please try not to freak out."

Malorie held her hands up in a placating manner, or perhaps to try to get as much distance between her and Anne as possible. She couldn't deny that she was a little scared of how Anne would react and although it seemed Anne could not physically harm her, as she was incorporeal, she was still afraid of the havoc she could likely still wreak. The cold wind-blowy thing she did might not be the only trick that ancient ghosts could pull off, but Malorie couldn't say for certain.

"Soooo… you were executed in 1536 on the orders of Henry VIII." Thank God she had listened to her dad's latest history lesson on Queen Anne so she could inform her of all this. "It is currently the year 2019," she continued.

She paused to let Anne process her words. Anne seemed to pale even more, which was saying a lot considering how pallid her skin was to begin with. Her eyes were wide, and it was clear she would be wringing her hands if her immaterial form would allow her to.

2019? She asked as though it were a foreign word she was having trouble pronouncing. She dragged out each syllable as if she were a toddler just learning to speak. *Surely, you jest. Surely that year cannot exist. I am not a fool to be convinced of futuristic children's stories, girl*, she said, throwing a lot of contempt behind the word 'girl,' which Malorie was not a fan of. *It is the year 1536. It is May. My dear brother, George, has just been killed*. At this, her voice tightened as if she were holding back a sob. She continued, *Do you think I have lost my wits? How could you suggest something so foolish as 2019?* Again, she dragged out the number as if it were a foreign concept that she simply couldn't wrap her tongue around.

"Just look around, Anne—" Malorie started but she was quickly cut off.

Do not presume to call me by my Christian name, girl. You may address me as Your Majesty, Anne declared.

Wow, rude! Why did Malorie think it was such a good idea to help such a mean lady again?

Malorie was in no mood to pick fights, so she simply continued, "Look around, Your Majesty." She made a grand flourish with her arm outstretched, encompassing the whole room. "Does any of this look familiar to you? Have you ever seen a pillow made out of, um, whatever the heck this fuzzy stuff is?" she asked as she held up the hot pink pillow in question.

"Or what about this?" she asked as she pressed the power button on her remote to turn the flat screen TV perched on her wall on. Anne jumped back in fright and momentarily disappeared through Malorie's dresser as a rerun of *Friends* appeared on the screen.

"And if that's not enough, I think this one is *sure* to convince you you're in the future," Malorie exclaimed as she pulled her cell phone from her pocket and pulled up YouTube.

There are tiny, moving people on this tiny device. And what is this caterwauling? Anne asked. Malorie had pulled up the last video she had watched which happened to be an Ariana Grande music video. By Anne's mentioning of caterwauling, Malorie had to assume she wasn't a fan.

This is clearly witchcraft! How have you avoided being burned alive?! I must speak to Henry at once! He will set this right, Anne said as she spun on her heel and attempted to leave. Malorie tried to grab her wrist and pull her back which only left her with icy fingers.

"No, no, Your Majesty. It's not witchcraft. It's the future. This is how technology has progressed. I know that's a lot to take in. I'm sorry. I wish

I could take things slower and introduce you to the future one device at a time so you don't die a second death, if that's even possible, but we don't have time. I think you were brought back to the future because I touched your necklace. I think your spirit is attached to this necklace and I think your spirit has finally been able to leave the Tower because your necklace has," Malorie said, holding up the necklace in question.

Anne tried to reach for it once more and her fingers slid right through it. Malorie saw shock, pain, and fear flash in Anne's eyes all at once.

Why can I not grab this thing? Hand me mine own jewels now. No more games!

Malorie could tell she was getting flustered the longer she spoke. She knew Anne needed to rage a little longer and take some more time to really process the state, place, and year she was in. Malorie was sure she'd be reacting the same way if she had just found out she was a spirit waking up nearly 500 years after she thought she'd died. "I'm so sorry," Malorie spoke softly.

How is my spirit still on this earth? I thought God wouldst judge me accordingly and send mine own soul to heaven, Anne replied, with a note of despair in her voice.

Anne's talk of God and heaven reminded Malorie that she *was* a religious woman, just as all of Henry's queens were according to her dad, although probably still not quite as pious as Katherine of Aragon. Malorie couldn't imagine how hard it would be to grapple not only with the concept of being in a strange place and strange time but also with not ending up where you thought God would take you.

"Do you have some sort of unfinished business here?" Malorie asked tentatively; she didn't want to spook Anne any more than she was already spooked. "Perhaps your soul can't go to heaven until you resolve something here on earth?" That's how it always played out in movies and TV shows. Of course she knew the media wasn't real so that method might not actually work, but hey, she didn't think ghosts were real until a few hours ago. She supposed anything was worth a try.

The last thing I remember thinking was that I wouldst make Henry pay for what he'd done, Anne replied. Malorie was glad to see that Anne had finally calmed down enough to answer her questions. She seemed to be focusing all of her energy on conversing with Malorie, and Malorie had a feeling it was because she didn't want to see more futuristic things and send her mind reeling with shock any further. Things would be better if they could speak to each other rationally. Which was a bizarre concept considering the person she was speaking rationally to was a ghost, but, nevertheless.

Tell me, what happened to Henry? How didst he die? Anne asked, and Malorie was surprised to hear how much care and concern she could sense in her voice. She supposed she would be feeling a lot of conflicting emotions too for a man who had once loved her so dearly only to send her to the chopping block a few years later when he was ready to move on. She supposed she was grateful that boys nowadays just ended relationships with cruelly written text messages. It seemed like a much better ending than death.

"I... I don't know. I'm sorry. I'm not the history buff around here, my dad is. He could tell you!" Malorie answered excitedly. Although the excitement immediately turned sour in her belly as she considered just how hard it would be to try to explain to her dad that she had a ghost living in her pocket now.

Admittedly, she felt terrible that she couldn't provide Anne with more answers, but she felt confident they would get those answers soon and resolve the problem of her lingering spirit.

"So, you want revenge on Henry?" Malorie continued. "That's fair. I can help you and maybe put your spirit to rest. But, for now, although I can't imagine how I'll do it, I have to try to get some rest. We have a long day ahead of us tomorrow." And with that she placed the necklace on her bedside table and watched Anne dissipate in a gray mist. A sense of calm washed over her now that the room was silent and warm again. She lay down, shut her eyes, and let sleep overtake her.

CHAPTER FIVE

January 1536

Anne paced by the window, anxiously wringing her hands. Anger flared deep within her and she felt the babe kick as if he protested too. How could Henry do this to her? He knew how fragile she was, not just in body with the ever-growing babe in her stomach, but in mind. She knew her situation was precarious, knew there were hundreds of people in court who despised her, most prominent of all being Thomas Cromwell, but she *had* to succeed, she *had* to keep going. How dare Henry make that harder for her by bouncing the plain whore Jane Seymour on his lap?

Was it because Jane was demure where Anne was outspoken? Henry insisted she keep her thoughts to herself but how could she when he flirted with that Jane whore plain as day for anyone to see? *She* was queen and she needed everyone to know it. They might start doubting if they saw him blatantly flirt with Jane as he had once blatantly flirted with Anne before the eyes of the now Dowager Princess of Wales, Katherine of Aragon, and her court.

She needed Henry to trust in her. Trust that the babe currently growing in her belly was the heir he needed, trust that she was doing good for this country with the reformation she led, and, above all, trust that God smiled on their union. But he made trust so hard when she could see plain as day that he didn't trust her. If he had, he wouldn't already be looking for the next woman to fill his marriage bed and give him a son.

She thought she had his ear above all others, but she could see that the poisonous words that Thomas Cromwell was whispering were starting to take root in Henry's mind. He had become ever more fickle with age and was so easily swayed. But no matter, she just had to sway him back to her side. And she knew she could. Nobody else would have his ear once she gave him a son. The babe kicked in that moment as if in affirmation.

"Your Majesty, the Duke of Norfolk is here to see you," her lady-in-waiting, Margery, announced.

"See him in," Anne grumbled, still lost in thought over her musings about Henry.

Anne hardly had a chance to finish her sentence before the Duke of Norfolk was rushing in, breathing heavily as if he had run fast and hard from a very long distance.

"Your Majesty, I regret to inform you but, there has been an incident. His Majesty is gravely injured," the duke announced soberly.

Anne clutched at the chair in front of her until her knuckles turned white. Her legs quickly gave out and she found herself clutching at the rug before her, sobbing. She had never lost control like this. She had always kept herself calm and collected, even in front of her uncle, but she had no control over her actions in this moment. Her Henry, the man she both loved yet feared, the man who infuriated her as much as he delighted her, was on death's doorway and there was nothing she could do.

How could she move forward if he died? Without a known male heir produced from her womb, the succession would soon leave her behind. And she would not be safe if his daughter, Mary, took the throne. Mary despised Anne and would just as soon have her imprisoned in the tower or sent off to a nunnery.

No, Anne was not safe without Henry. She was barely safe with him, but without Henry, her grip on this court would slip right through her fingers. She needed him to live, for the safety of herself and for the realm.

She wailed once more, let out a few deep breaths, composing herself, before asking, "What happened?"

"His Majesty was in the midst of a jousting tournament when he fell from his horse and gravely wounded his leg," the duke answered.

Anne took a few more deep breaths before asking, "My Lord, what are his chances for a recovery?"

"It is uncertain at this time, Your Majesty. He has been unconscious now for many hours. But his body has responded well to the leeching, so there is hope yet," the duke answered once more.

Anne, who had risen and composed herself in order to speak with her uncle, found herself collapsing to the floor once more as she was seized by a torturously painful cramp in her belly.

"Ahhhhh," she cried out in pain. Her maids rushed to her side at once, grabbing her arms and attempting to lift her once more.

"Uncle, send for the physician at once," she grunted through clenched teeth. She was amazed she could speak at all for the pain was so great.

"But, Your Majesty, the physician is currently attending the King," the duke answered. Concern was etched on his face, but he sounded puzzled, as if no matter how great her pain, nobody dared take the King's physician away from him.

"I do not care. Send someone to tend to me NOW, my lord, or you will soon find you have no king to serve," Anne shouted, crying out in pain on her last word. The venom that laced her tone was so potent, the duke dared not question her order again. He raced out of the room, and she prayed he'd bring her salvation.

Anne's tears peppered her bedsheets as she felt the sticky substance between her legs that she could only imagine was blood. Her sweat slicked hand gripped her lady Elizabeth's hand as pain lanced through her belly. She could hear the physician at the foot of the bed speaking to her in soothing tones, but she couldn't make out what he was saying. Nothing existed for her right now but pain. The last thing she was conscious of was the heat between her legs and the fear that flooded her brain as the bleeding continued ever more profusely.

Anne awoke with her head pounding. Bleary-eyed, she reached her trembling hand out to what appeared to be a human form by her bedside. "Water," she croaked. If she were of sound mind, she'd despise the way she sounded so weak. But her wits were not about her as she parted her parched lips to sip the cool, refreshing water placed before her.

After a few moments, she managed to recollect herself and she realized she was surrounded by her ladies-in-waiting, Lady Margery and Lady Elizabeth.

"What happened?" she croaked, voice still hoarse from lack of water and a fair amount of screaming.

"Your Majesty, there had been a jousting incident with His Grace and, well, unfortunately, the stress of the incident caused–"

Margery had no chance to finish her sentence because in that moment, Anne appeared to finally recognize just how flat her stomach was as she screamed, "My babe! Where has he gone? What happened?"

Anne frantically pulled up her dressing gown as if a bouncing, baby boy would suddenly appear between her legs. When she was met with nothing but red-stained sheets, she openly wept.

"My boy! Where has he gone?" she asked again, wailing for the second time in as many days. She clutched her stomach as if she could bring her babe back and hold him inside of her once more.

"Your Grace, that is what we've been sent to tell you," Elizabeth answered. She grasped Anne's hand as gently as possible as she continued, "His Majesty, King Henry suffered a horrible jousting accident a few days ago. We believe the stress of this news caused you to miscarry. The physician did all he could to save the child, but ultimately, you were delivered of a stillborn boy."

Anne couldn't stop the tears from streaming down her face. Her son, and with him, her hopes and dreams for the future were dead. She had failed time and time again and now Henry would see no choice before him but to be rid of her. That was if Henry still lived.

"And Henry? How does he fair?" Anne asked.

"We are very fortunate that His Grace will make a full recovery!" Lady Margery beamed proudly. "He has regained consciousness. His physicians have been waiting on him hand and foot. He has been informed of your condition and he has been beside himself with grief. He has been ordered to rest and recover for a few days, from the incident as well as this latest news," Margery finished solemnly.

"I must see him," Anne replied. She attempted to sit up in bed but was quickly winded by the motion as pain lanced through her body. In that moment, her physician entered bearing a cup with a strange concoction.

"You must rest, Your Majesty," he said as he brought the cup to her lips. "This will help with the pain and allow you some sleep. You will make a full recovery in a few days' time. For now, you must rest."

Visions of her babe and Henry succumbing to horrible pain plagued her mind as she drifted off to sleep.

Anne awoke to the sound of birds chirping and sunlight shining on her face. Lady Elizabeth rushed into the room as soon as she heard Anne's rustling. "My lady, what is it?" Elizabeth asked.

"What day is it? May I see Henry now?" she asked brusquely. She was tired of bedrest, tired of reliving the trauma of losing her babe. She needed to walk, she needed to confront Henry. She was afraid she might go stir-crazy if she did not.

"Your Grace, it has been three days since both you and His Grace have been bedridden. His Majesty has awoken and has been attending to affairs. He will allow you to see him now," Lady Elizabeth said.

"Good. Fetch me my clothes," Anne answered.

"Her Majesty Queen Anne Boleyn is here to see you, my lord," Henry's attendant announced as he opened the wide, mahogany doors.

Henry hardly had a chance to reply before Anne pounced on him.

"How could you frighten me like that?" she asked, her voice flushed as she embraced him.

She trembled in his arms and after a moment, Henry pulled away from her, saying, "Oh, my dear Nan. Are you okay?" He gingerly placed a hand on her flat stomach, a delicate expression gleaming in his eyes, like he had all the care in the world for her.

She anticipated anger seeping from this man and instead she was met with kindness. Perhaps he was still too shocked from his own brush with death to be very angry towards her. Perhaps he *did* still care about her and had truly feared for her life.

"I am much better now," she answered. "Although I lost–"

Her voice choked with emotion and she could not bring herself to finish the sentence.

"I know, my sweet, I know," Henry said. His voice was soft, but his eyes had hardened, and Anne could see the anger brewing within. Perhaps she was not wrong to think that this loss might be the last straw for him.

She pulled away. She could not bear for him to lay all the blame at her feet.

"You know, tis not my fault. The stress of your fall caused me to lose the babe," she started. "You nearly died, and I could not live without you. How could our son and I survive without you? It was too much to bear." She braced herself against an ornate chair, eyes downcast at the mere thought of losing the king. A tear trickled down her cheek.

"You cause me so much grief, you know," she cried. "You commit outrageous acts that nearly kill you *and* you flaunt the Seymour wench right under my nose! Why must you hurt me?" she asked, tears streaking her cheeks once more.

"That is enough!" Henry shouted. "What I do with the women in my court is my business! You had best learn to hold your tongue, Mistress Anne. I raised you this high and I can lower you just as fast," he growled, anger lacing his words.

"I am your Queen!" Anne retorted. "I am your wife and the mother of your child. How could you debase me so?"

"Men take mistresses. *Kings* take mistresses. I am appointed by God, and I can damn well do as I please."

"I carried your son and still you'd humiliate me?" Anne cried. She was beginning to lose her resolve in the face of his anger. She could not stand to see him treat her so.

"You do not carry my son any longer," Henry answered, glancing at her flat stomach before turning on his heel and storming out of the room.

Anne let out a sob. If that was where his mind was then she knew her fate was as good as sealed.

CHAPTER SIX

◈

August 2019

Malorie awoke to the warmth of the sun caressing her face and the smell of pancakes wafting from the other room. She beamed widely, a gleam of mischievousness and excitement in her eyes. It was her last day in London and clearly her dad wanted to send her out with a bang.

And then the memory of the visit to the Tower of London, Anne's ghost, the necklace, and the late-night revenge conversation all hit her like a ton of bricks and knocked the air right out of her chest. She felt like ice water was coursing through her veins as she glanced over to the necklace on her bedside table and remembered that all she had to do was touch it and the nightmare she'd been living in all day yesterday would continue.

It chilled her not only because she was afraid to summon Anne's ghost and continue this whole ordeal, but because she knew she had to in order to find any sense of peace or sanity ever again. And what was worse was that she knew she'd have to involve her dad. There was no way she could answer Anne's questions without him.

She glanced at the passport and boarding pass lying on top of her dresser and an anxious knot formed in her stomach. This trip had been planned for months and that ticket was the key to the life she longed to get back to. She couldn't just throw her normal, American life away because she'd developed conflicting feelings and a hero complex for a ghost, could she? Because there was no way around having to extend her trip if she *did* decide to help Anne. She couldn't very well solve this problem from America.

But why should she solve this problem at all? Sure, a part of her feared for the next person Anne might haunt, but Malorie was just a kid and she never asked for the necklace or the ghost attached to it! She'd barely asked for any of the items London had offered her thus far. Would it really be so selfish of her to toss the necklace in the garbage before heading to the airport? She'd just *assumed* the necklace had some magic properties that would allow it to keep haunting people, but for all she knew, she could send it on its way to the dump and nobody would ever know the necklace/ghost existed. She was just a kid after all and taking on this kind of responsibility was way above her pay grade! She gnawed on her bottom lip as she worried over the choices before her.

She had long had an adventurous spirit and her courageous heart was pulling her to embark on this adventure. Her friends and family would still be waiting for her when she got home but this was a once in a lifetime opportunity. Plus, Malorie had never met a puzzle she couldn't solve. Her mom used to call her Sherlock Holmes because she was so invested in reading Nancy Drew books and solving mysteries. And the need to solve this puzzle was weighing on her too.

But she had a whole new set of worries that had nothing to do with whether her friends would be able to meet her at the mall when she got home. How was she going to tell her dad 1) that she wanted to stay in London (if that's what she decided to do) and 2) that she could give him the opportunity to speak with and help out Anne Boleyn without sounding like an absolute nutcase? (Sounding crazy was exactly why she had already ruled out taking this to the police.) She couldn't even guarantee that he would be able to see Anne. Maybe *she* was the only one with the power to see Anne? If that were the case, she wouldn't just *sound* like a nutcase, she'd actually be one. She supposed she just had to get it over with and have this conversation with him once and for all.

"Morning, love," her dad greeted her as he set a plate full of pancakes in front of her seat at the kitchen table. "I made sure to get some of that too sweet syrup you Americans like," he chuckled before placing a bottle on the table. Although her dad was born and raised in America just like

Malorie, he considered himself more of a Londoner after getting his dual citizenship and living here for over a decade. "Dig in," he continued and sat across from her.

Malorie sat in silence for a few moments, watching the syrup drip off of a freshly doused pancake. She didn't know how to form the words for what she needed to tell him. She dug into the pancakes slowly, but each bite felt like chewing cardboard.

"Are you alright, love?" he asked. "You seem a little dazed. Did you get a good night's sleep? You know, you'll need it for the plane ride home today," he babbled, trying to fill the silence and, she sensed, trying to mask his sadness over having to say goodbye so soon after they'd just been reunited.

"I… I'm fine," she started hesitantly. *Okay, Malorie, just rip the Band-Aid off. Get it all out there so we can move forward with helping Anne.* "Um, but… I… I was wondering two things actually," she started.

Her dad gave her an encouraging look and the moment she saw the gleam in his eyes, she knew she could This is absolutely bonkers!" trust him with anything she said, and she knew he would have her back no matter what. That gleam in his eye told her that even if he couldn't see Anne like she could, he would go to the ends of the earth to help her on her mission. She was sure it was a matter of making up for lost time but regardless, she was finally insanely appreciative to have this papa bear of a protector looking out for her.

"I was wondering if I could stay here a little longer," she spit out rapidly. She had decided, maybe against her best interests, that she needed to help Anne. She may just be a teenager with no sense of how to break curses or aid ghosts, but she knew deep down that it was the right thing to do. If she had to flip a coin and it landed on "Heads for America", she'd be disappointed that she hadn't stayed and helped. She knew he would question her decision considering she hadn't hidden her feelings about not being pleased to be here in the first place, but everything had changed when Anne materialized into her life. She had to convince him that staying was the best option for her right now.

"You really want to, love? I honestly didn't think you liked it here very much," her father said, a puzzled expression crossing his face. He looked a little disappointed that London, and by extension himself, might not be everything she'd hoped it would be. A part of her wanted to comfort him and wipe the sad look off of his face, but another thought he deserved to wallow since he brought this on himself.

"No, I love London. I could practically live here, it's just so fun," she said. She hoped she was doing a decent job of saving face, but she could hear the way her sweetness likely came across as sarcasm and based off of the curious expression in her father's eyes and the slight tilt of his head like he was a confused puppy dog, she doubted he was believing her words.

"I want to believe you, sweetie, believe me I do but... let's just say... your behavior over the course of the past week has led me to believe you're not so comfortable here. I'm sorry for that and believe me, I've done everything in my power to make you feel welcome. I really wanted to form a strong connection with you because I genuinely do regret leaving all of those years ago. I'm sorry I'm not what you wanted me to be," he finished his soliloquy with a downcast look and the glimmer of a tear in his eye.

In that moment, Malorie felt she should have put in more effort into pretending to have a good time this whole week. She might have been feeling disdain for her father, but she never meant to actually hurt his feelings. *Time for some reassurance, I guess,* she thought before saying, "No, no, it's nothing like that, Peter! I don't want you to feel bad and I should have been a better guest and daughter to you this whole time. Okay, the truth is I need to stay because I have some business to attend to. And I need your help."

Peter looked at her again with that confused puppy dog head tilt. "I'm not sure I'm following," he said.

"Can you just call mom and tell her my flight's been delayed or something?" Malorie pleaded.

"Well, what is this business, love? Saying you've got 'business' to attend to sounds a little dodgy. I won't do something that will put you in harm's way," her father choked out, his throat tightening in his effort to stay calm. He might not have known his daughter for very long, but he loved her dearly still and cared about her so very deeply.

"Dad, it's a good thing you're sitting down because it's a lot to unpack," she answered, pausing to take a slow bite of pancake in an effort to organize her thoughts.

"So... remember when I disappeared on you in Winchester Hall yesterday? Sorry about that again, by the way. Well, I came across a secret door that led me to a secret room. I know, I know. This sounds like something straight out of a fantasy novel but just stick with me for a sec. In the secret room I found this," she finished, and she pulled the necklace out of her jacket pocket with a flourish. She was careful to grab it with a handkerchief as she was not ready to bring Anne into the picture just yet.

You might think it odd, dear reader, that a sixteen-year-old is carrying around an object that is so far out of fashion that not even decrepit, old men tend to use it anymore, but the truth is that Malorie's father, being the oddball he is, insists on always carrying a handkerchief with him because 'it's a massively useful thing to have and has great practical value.' Malorie was pretty sure Peter saw handkerchiefs the way interstellar hitchhiker's saw towels, useful in any situation, and that was why he handed her one on her first day in London when she needed to wipe mud off of her pants. It had since been washed and was restored to its vibrant aubergine color. Malorie had scoffed at the idea of needing a handkerchief that first day and yet here she was, wrapping a necklace in it, so she supposed her father had been right after all

"That's... that's Anne Boleyn's necklace!" he choked out as Malorie tentatively unwrapped the handkerchief from around the precious jewel. He could barely get the words out in his excitement. "H... how... how could you possibly have this? No modern historian has ever been able to track it down! It was expected that it was passed on to Elizabeth I, but no one can say for certain. This is absolutely bonkers!"

His excitement was so palpable, she could taste it in the air. She'd never seen anyone's eyes become so large and shiny. She'd never seen passion written so plainly on someone's face. She locked eyes with him and knew that he'd have all the answers she'd need to help Anne.

"Can I? ... I have to..." he started and before she could process what was happening, his long fingers had curled around the closest pearl. He held the necklace in his hands like it was a newborn child he meant to cherish. He gazed at it adoringly.

He stared at the necklace so long Malorie was starting to think Anne might not appear to him, but then she saw his eyes glaze over in horror as he finally looked up and she knew Anne had appeared. She thought she might have even seen the hairs on his balding head sway a little as if a cool breeze caressed them upon Anne's arrival.

"I really wish you hadn't done that," Malorie mumbled. Her dad shrieked and dropped the necklace on the table. The clatter of the pearls on the hardwood was nearly lost as his scream intensified.

"Dad, please calm down," Malorie said in the most soothing voice she could muster. "It's going to be okay." She placed her hands on his and found they were cold to the touch, like all of the warmth had been drained out of him by Anne's appearance.

He gazed into Malorie's eyes, then stared around the room, stunned by the sudden disappearance of the apparition.

"Where?... What?... I think I just saw..." Peter stuttered out. He was still in shock and couldn't form complete sentences, so Malorie got up to start making him a cup of tea. If there was anything she had learned in the past week of living in London it was that tea fixed any situation.

"Dad, take a few deep breaths. Yes, you saw Anne Boleyn, yes, her spirit is attached to that necklace," Malorie continued, rummaging in the cupboards to find bags of tea after turning the stove on to heat the kettle. "She is the business I need to take care of and the reason I can't go home today. I know you might think we've just eaten something that's giving us bad hallucinations or something to that effect. Trust me, I tried every way to rationalize this last night. But the fact of the matter is, her spirit is attached to that necklace, and she won't find rest until she completes her mission. She wants revenge on Henry VIII, and I can't say I really blame her. But I can't help her like you can. I don't know her history or his as well as you do. Heck, I don't even know where Henry is buried! But I'm sure you do and that's why we need your help. Please," Malorie ended on an imploring note as she sat across from him and pushed a steaming cup of tea into his hands.

Her father continued to stare at her like she'd lost her mind, which was exactly what she had feared. Maybe she *had* lost her mind. Maybe she was too quick to accept the whole "ghosts are real and sometimes they have unfinished business" premise. Perhaps she had let too many TV shows sway her into thinking this was the proper course of action. Still, she plowed on.

"Dad, I know I sound crazy, but you have to believe me," she pleaded.

The necklace sat between them on the table and Peter had a look in his eyes that either said, "I want to cherish this necklace" or "I want to chuck it in the bin." Malorie wasn't sure which option was better. Knowing she had wanted to toss the necklace only moments before, she couldn't blame him for wanting the same thing. But they couldn't afford to throw this necklace away and have the next stranger be haunted. They couldn't guarantee that the next person would be able to help Anne like Peter could.

"Please, dad. It's important. We have to help Anne," she implored yet again. "From what I've gathered, she only appears when someone touches the necklace. I know this sounds crazy, but I held the necklace for a while last night and she told me her story. I know you already know her story but maybe if you hold the necklace and see her for longer than a few seconds, you'll believe in her and be willing to help me help her."

Her father finally gained his voice long enough to ask, "Why do you want to help her anyway? You made it clear you don't give a wig about history so what's changed? I would think someone so nonchalant would have no problem chucking this necklace in the bin and flying home to America. Why make this your problem," he said, gesturing to the necklace, "when it doesn't have to be?"

"I didn't care about history because it didn't feel real. It didn't have an effect on me. It was just some boring stuff that happened in the past to a bunch of boring people. But Anne feels real. She's real when I hold that necklace and she needs help!" Malorie stated emphatically. "She's a sad woman who wants to find some closure with the lover who spurned her. I can get that. I get relationships," Malorie said. She reflected on Robbie and his treatment of her lately. Perhaps once Malorie helped Anne find closure with Henry, Malorie might have to find her *own* closure with Robbie.

"Besides, we have to help her dad because we *can* help her! *You* can help her! If we toss this necklace away and pretend she never appeared to us, who's to say the cursed necklace won't reappear somewhere else? Who's to say she won't haunt someone else? Who's to say that new person will be able to help her? What if she continues to haunt and suffer because we didn't do anything?" Malorie asked.

"You know, for a teenager you really are wise beyond your years," Peter joked nervously, eyeing the necklace with trepidation.

"I know you don't want to believe me. Heck, I'm still not sure if *I* even believe me. I'm still processing this all just like you. And I know I'm just a silly teenager. I know you'll probably try to come up with every excuse imaginable to explain why what you just saw isn't real because I did the same thing. But I think we should try to believe what we saw. I'm trusting my gut and my gut says to help Anne," Malorie finished and pushed the necklace towards Peter. "Give Anne a chance to tell you her story fresh, from her own point of view. If you see her for more than two seconds, I'm sure you'll believe in her. Please, dad," Malorie entreated.

That last please and the look Peter saw in Malorie's eyes was enough to convince him that he had to give her a chance. Gingerly, he picked up the necklace. It almost looked like he clutched the pearls tighter in his fist as his hair blew back and Malorie was certain Anne had reappeared to him.

He sat motionless, wide-eyed, and slack jawed as, she assumed, Anne told him her story. Occasionally he'd pepper in questions, but Malorie tuned him out. She wasn't interested in participating at the moment, she had been through this whole experience once before and once was one time too many for her. She was still eagerly awaiting the moment things went back to normal for her.

After maybe ten minutes her dad set the necklace down, stood up, and poured himself a shot of whiskey. Malorie bit her knuckle in an attempt to stifle a laugh.

After a couple more refills, her dad sat back down and simply stated, "Okay, I believe you. And you're right, we have to help her. I don't know exactly where we'll find Henry's ghost but I'm a world-renowned Tudor historian so if anyone can do it, it's me!" Peter quipped.

Again with the jokes? Malorie thought. He must be more nervous than she thought. But he was on board and that was all that mattered. Together, they would solve Anne's problem and lay her spirit to rest.

"Good. Now that everyone is on board, I think our only option right now is to bring Anne back," she said, casting a quick glance at the necklace, "and come up with a plan. But first, let's call the airline and cancel my flight."

CHAPTER SEVEN

"Well, your mum is confused, a little angry, and certainly worried about your decision but I finally got her to agree to let you stay for another week," Peter said as he snapped his cell phone shut (yes, he was one of those weird, middle-aged men who still used a flip phone) and walked back into the kitchen. Relief poured through Malorie. She was almost certain she was going to end up on the phone call begging and pleading, or having her mom make her feel guilty by asking, "Don't you miss your friends? Don't you miss me?" She could only process so many emotions right now and the prime emotions on her brain lately had been fear of Anne and concern for Anne.

With that out of the way it didn't take long before Anne, Malorie, and her dad were chatting around the kitchen table like old friends. Malorie was having a hard time processing the fact that her dad went from screaming bloody murder maybe twenty minutes ago to now being deeply engrossed in a conversation with a ghost, but to each their own, Malorie supposed.

In the back of her mind, Malorie realized she'd never be able to tell her mom or friends any of this when she got back home. She'd be committed to an institution if she did. Malorie glanced over to see the spark of joy in her father's eyes as he chatted with Anne like she was an old friend stopping by for tea and not a 500-year-old phantom queen. It took all of her energy not to chuckle to herself. She still had a hard time believing all of this was really happening.

Malorie tuned back into the conversation just in time to hear Anne ask the question she had asked last night that Malorie had no answer for: *Tell me, what happened to Henry? How didst he die?* In this moment she was beyond grateful that her father was a highly educated historian and, not only that, but a historian who had devoted his *life* to Tudor history so he could answer this question and get them started down the road of hopefully putting Anne's spirit to rest.

"While the true cause of his death isn't known, there have been many theories tossed out over the centuries. Septic infection, scurvy, endocrine disease, venous hypertension, and syphilis are all possible killers - although syphilis is unlikely as he wasn't treated for it, nor did he pass the symptoms along to his children. Ultimately, he never fully recovered from his jousting accident that badly ulcerated his legs. He had become obese and never regained the health of his youth. He died in 1547."

Ha! From the jousting accident that caused me such stress that I lost my babe. He deserved a gruesome death like he gave me, Anne responded. There was so much malice in her voice. Malorie shouldn't be surprised considering all that she knew about Anne now. She had seen the cold, calculating blaze in Anne's eyes when she thought of what Henry had done to her and knew she'd never want to be on the receiving end of it.

Malorie glanced over to her father to see a glimmer of sadness in his eye. She supposed he, too, could understand the mixed emotions Anne must be feeling and how much a heart could hurt when someone you once loved turned on you so quickly. Maybe he'd felt something similar with her mother.

Anne continued, asking, *Didst he suffer long?* Malorie was amazed at the way her voice suddenly dripped sickly sweet with concern. She felt like she was getting whiplash from Anne's mercurial moods and the speed with which they changed. Yet, she supposed she shouldn't be surprised that Anne could feel two very strong, very conflicting emotions juxtaposed together. From what she'd heard, Henry was clearly a man of passion and Malorie realized that passion could take the positive form of love or the negative form of hate. And, she supposed, the two could switch easily at the flip of a dime in someone as mentally unstable as Henry seemed to be. So what choice did Anne have but to try to keep up with his ever-changing moods?

"He did. He was on the verge of death for many months," her father answered. And as thrilled as Anne seemed to be at the thought of Henry dying gruesomely, she now had a shadow of sadness cross her face like she wished for anything *but* an end like that for Henry.

If Malorie could read Anne's mind, she'd understand that while Anne's emotions seemed to teeter between the two extremes of love and hate on the outside, internally Anne was feeling a wide range of emotions and her facial expressions simply couldn't keep up with all she was feeling. If Malorie were a mind reader, she'd know that, yes, Anne was angry with Henry, of course she was. Not just for his betrayal, but for making her fall in love with him in the first place. Anne hadn't wanted his attention; she had even spurned his advances at first. But he began to make her feel like she truly was the only woman in the world he'd ever love. So, when his eyes started straying to Jane Seymour, Anne had been filled with jealousy, of course, but hate too. Anne hated him for lying and if he were any other man, she would have wanted to see him burn. But since he was the king and that wish could not come true, it had filled her with another emotion: fear. Anne knew what Henry could put his mind to with the right provocation; he could create a whole new church when things didn't go his way so what would he do to her if he felt she was in his way? And underneath it all lied guilt. Anne felt guilty for failing in her duty to provide a son. And as angry as she was with Henry, she was angry with herself as well, knowing that they wouldn't be caught in this entanglement of emotions if she could have just done her duty by him from the start.

And didst he e'er beget the son he wanted? she asked. Malorie would never have imagined she could hear so much pain in a ghost's voice, but then again, she never imagined she would hear a ghost speak at all. Unshed tears pooled in Anne's eyes and Malorie knew the unasked question that lingered on her tongue: *was there someone less broken than me who managed to succeed where I failed?*

Malorie couldn't have known it, but her father paused before answering as he contemplated, should he tell her about the other four wives? Well, three, really because she already knew about Jane Seymour. Would it destroy her to learn that Henry had married Jane just eleven days after her own death? Probably not, as she had already seen him moving so quickly in his flirtations with Jane while Anne was still living. But still, her body hadn't even lain cold in the ground for a fortnight before *his* body lain warm with a new woman. And if that didn't hurt her, he was sure the news that Jane Seymour gave birth to the boy Henry wanted so badly and that Anne could not conceive would wound her deeply.

He supposed the truth would only add more fodder to her desire for revenge on Henry, but perhaps it still was what she needed to hear to find peace with the situation. He thought she deserved to know the whole truth before confronting Henry, so he answered, "Henry married Jane Seymour eleven days after your execution," he started. He could already see the pain brimming in her eyes, but with it was a cold, hard anger and a fierce determination.

Carry on, she urged, her voice tight with her wrath.

"She bore him a son on October 12, 1537. They named him Edward. She died shortly afterwards due to complications from the birth," Peter answered gravely.

Didst the boy live? Anne asked next. Malorie could sense the fear and desperation in her voice. She was desperate to know that even if this woman had succeeded in producing a male heir, she had failed in keeping him alive. It was a cruel thought, may God have mercy on her soul, but she needed to know that it was all Henry's fault. She couldn't stand to think that maybe her body was a broken temple that couldn't house a baby in its womb. She had wanted to place all the blame on Henry but maybe it truly was her fault. She uttered a heart wrenching sob.

"Are... are you sure you want me to answer that?" Peter responded. It was obvious Anne was in pain and he didn't want to make things worse for her.

I need to know, she insisted.

"He did. But not for very long. Well, long enough to succeed Henry as King, but not for much longer after that. He succeeded Henry to the throne at age nine and died at age fifteen of what we now know was tuberculosis."

And what of mine own dear Elizabeth? Didst she e'er rule England like I dreamt she would? Anne asked, hope renewed in her voice.

"She did. She ruled for 45 years after her half-sister, Mary, passed in 1558." Anne flinched upon hearing the name Mary and it was clear she did not like hearing her daughter's name associated with the woman who caused her nothing but misery when she wouldn't acknowledge Anne as queen. That evil girl and her mother were Anne's greatest undoing. Too many people stayed loyal to her, and Anne wished she could have foreseen that before attempting her rise to power.

Anne remembered thinking once about Mary, "She is my death and I am hers; so I will take care that she shall not laugh at me after my death." Anne wondered whether Mary's spirit still remained on this earth as hers did. Or was Mary laughing from heaven as Anne wasted away in Purgatory? Her jaw clenched at the mere notion of Mary getting in the last laugh and she hoped she could find her way to Henry and ruin him like the wretch deserved before ascending into heaven.

Peter pulled her out of her reverie by continuing, "Her reign was hotly debated but many believed it to be one of the greatest reigns in English history. Protestantism prospered under her rule, she oversaw many expeditions, and overall, she was much loved. Unlike Mary who caused much bloodshed and terror during her reign as she sought to execute Protestants and instill Catholicism as the proper religion."

Anne seethed upon hearing about Mary's reign but the look of pure joy and adoration on her face upon hearing about Elizabeth was wonderful to see. Peter wondered if Anne was proud of Elizabeth for prospering the reformist faith as Anne herself strived to do during her reign. He thought it'd be best if he didn't bring up the fact that Mary had Elizabeth imprisoned for part of her reign as the look of anger in her eyes every time Mary was even mentioned made it clear Anne would be ready to exact revenge on another person if given the chance.

And her kin? Anne continued. *Didst she marry the Dauphin of France like I wanted her to?*

"Sadly, Elizabeth never married. Nor did she have any children. But she did have many suitors! She was known to be quite the charming young woman in the height of her reign and was said to have flirted with and persuaded many dignitaries and marriage prospects to garner much support for herself throughout her reign," Peter answered.

A smile lit Anne's face. No doubt, she was pleased to hear that her daughter managed to master her skill for flirtation and charm even though Anne herself didn't have a chance to pass it down to her.

She turned out to be quite the accomplished woman. I couldn't be happier to hear how well she fared despite the terror of the first few years of her life, Anne said with a smile.

Peter was so happy to see the way Anne was beaming with pride; he didn't have the heart to tell her that Elizabeth's terror did not end upon Anne's death. How could he face this mother who just wanted to know her daughter had been okay and tell her that the daughter in question had actually been imprisoned by her half-sister for much of that sister's reign as queen? He couldn't, and luckily, he didn't have to because Anne soon asked, *Can you tell me more about her suitors? I'd like to know of the men who might have captured my daughter's heart if she had given them the chance. I need to know if they were worthy of her.*

Peter was all too happy to answer this question, which diverted him from having to tell Anne about her daughter's teen years. "She was quickly courted by Philip II of Spain after her reign began."

Bah! Of Spain!? Anne interjected. *I'm sure he has relations to the wench, Katherine of Aragon? He was likely Catholic, too! I'm glad Elizabeth spurned him. He was no match for her.*

"You're right!" Peter agreed. "He was Catholic, and Katherine was his great aunt. To make matters worse, he was married to Elizabeth's sister, Mary, first!" Peter exclaimed.

Bah! Anne shouted yet again and flinched once more at hearing Mary's name on Peter's lips. *What a knave! Speak no more of him. He was no match for Elizabeth. Who were her other suitors?* Anne asked.

"Two of the most appealing prospects from Elizabeth's counsellor's perspectives were King Eric XIV of Sweden and James Hamilton, 3rd Earl of Arran," Peter answered. "They were both Protestant which greatly increased their appeal to Elizabeth and her counselors. James was especially well liked because a union between the two of them would have secured an Anglo-Scottish alliance for the pair. She kept both of them on a string until around 1560 when she sent out letters rejecting their advances."

Peter saw sadness reflected in Anne's eyes at that comment, likely because she was sad for what Elizabeth lost by not marrying, especially to a decent suitor. Peter thought he might cheer her up by mentioning another suitor Anne would not approve of.

"Perhaps I can interest you in hearing about another suitor who you likely would not have approved of for Elizabeth," Peter said. He meant to say it lightheartedly, but Anne was giving him a glare that said, *Don't presume to tell me what I do and don't want to hear!* However, all she said was, ***Proceed***, and Peter breathed a sigh of relief knowing he was in the clear for now.

"Well, she was also courted by Archduke Charles of Austria. Charles was said to be quite handsome with dark, brooding eyes, but he was Catholic, so Elizabeth never took the courtship too seriously. After about a year, she rejected his advances too."

Anne looked gloomy again, likely at the thought of Elizabeth's rejections. She was afraid her daughter had never known love and what kind of way was that to live!?

Peter continued, "Don't think Elizabeth spurned all of her suitors so harshly. She had one suitor, Francois, Duc d'Anjou—"

Excellent, a French match, Anne interjected, her eyes alight with pleasure for her daughter's fortune, despite knowing that none of these dalliances panned out.

"Yes, a French match," Peter continued. "A French match that Elizabeth's advisors were not a fan of as they anticipated riots amongst the people over an Anglo-French alliance.

"Despite that, Francois was one of Elizabeth's most persistent suitors and even visited her in person during the courtship. It was clear that Elizabeth was quite fond of him though they were only ever friends," Peter said.

Before Anne could display a glum look on her face, Peter decided he'd end this suitor discussion by mentioning the most controversial yet most beloved by Elizabeth: Robert Dudley.

"And lastly, there was Robert Dudley," Peter explained. "Believed by nearly every Tudor historian to be someone Elizabeth was actually in love with."

At this, Anne perked up and the gleam returned to her eye. Finally, some good news about Elizabeth's love life. ***So, she did know love? I am happy for her. Love can be cruel, but it can also be the most pleasant feeling in the world,*** Anne proclaimed. Anne knew all too well how simultaneously kind and wicked love could be. She'd known too much heartache in her young life.

Peter agreed, then continued, "Dudley was not well liked by Elizabeth's advisors. No one was exactly pleased that he grew so high in the ranks so quickly. Upon Elizabeth's accession, she made Dudley Master of the

Horse. Though she loved him dearly, she never seriously considered the prospect of marriage because for one, he was already married and two, she knew marrying an Englishman would not be beneficial towards acquiring any alliances and would, more likely, lead to division of factions in England and possibly, civil war."

I am so sorry she was never able to marry for love. It seems to be a fate we both shared, Anne said, sadly. Peter was sure she was referring to her courtship and almost marriage to Henry Percy, heir to the earl of Northumberland. Peter knew they had been madly in love, but this occurred while King Henry VIII was falling in love with Anne himself, so he quickly put an end to the engagement.

Anne continued, *I tire of all this sad business of suitors gone sour. Tell me more of her reign!*

'She proudly reigned as the Virgin Queen until the end of her years. Many believe, and this is of course widely contested as no one in this day and age has the capability of getting into Elizabeth's mind, but many believe that she feared childbirth for the likely death that so often ensued, and she feared marriage for the way her father's marriages always failed," Peter said.

He continued, "The Tudor line ended with her, and the throne went to James I, the son of Mary, Queen of Scots. Mary was Henry VIII's great niece." Peter paused to take a sip of his tea before acknowledging, "I'm so sorry to be throwing all of these names at you all at once, it must be hard to follow."

Not at all. I am grateful to learn of mine own daughter's fate. I am glad life turned out better for her than it didst for me, Anne sighed, a hint of longing in her voice, likely for the daughter she never got to see grow up. Although possibly for the future heirs that Elizabeth couldn't bear to bring into existence.

"There is some more news you should probably know regarding Henry," Peter continued tentatively. "He married three more times after Jane Seymour died from birth complications. He married the German Anne of Cleves in January 1540, your cousin Katherine Howard in July 1540, and Catherine Parr in 1543," Peter stated.

Anne bristled at this news. *And didst any of these women receive a fate as cruel as mine?* Anne asked.

"Henry divorced Anne of Cleves claiming she was 'too ugly', to put it in modern terms. She was compliant to the divorce and from then until her death in 1557 she was considered the 'King's Sister' and treated with respect. Katherine Howard did not receive quite as decent of a fate. She was executed for adultery and treason, much like you. And like you, due to rumors of affairs she was having with the king's men. Catherine Parr outlived the king and died in 1548," Peter explained. "If it's any consolation to you though, all three women took wonderful care of your daughter, Elizabeth," Peter continued.

Anne's expression went to one of pure disgust and rage upon hearing the fates of the wives who succeeded her to one of genuine affection when learning further about her daughter's wellbeing.

Malorie made a show of looking at her watch and making a pointedly loud yawn. She was glad to be learning all of this history, especially as it seemed more like reality TV drama rather than some boring politics or war or something, but she knew they were on a timetable. It was great for her dad to be able to catch Anne up on Henry's life after her, but they didn't have the time to play catch up. They needed to find Henry to set things right. And they needed to do it as soon as possible with the tight deadline she was on.

When her yawn didn't catch the attention of her father or Anne, she said, "Weeeelll, while this info dump has been wonderful and all, can we get on with the mission? We have a king's ghost to summon and some closure to be found." She continued, "So while this conversation has been enlightening and I'm all for learning about some royal drama, we need to track down Henry. Dad, can you tell us where Henry is buried? I think that's probably the best place to start."

CHAPTER EIGHT

After hastily clearing the kitchen of teacups and leftover pancakes, Malorie and Peter found themselves on their way to St. George's Chapel. Anne's necklace was carefully wrapped in Peter's fancy purple handkerchief that Malorie was still borrowing and rested in Malorie's pocket. She didn't think it would look too good if her and her father were chatting up a ghost on the underground so thought it best to keep Anne tucked away for now. Not that they really needed to take the underground in the first place, Peter had merely decided early on in their week together that they were going to do this tourist thing the right way, so he had insisted on purchasing train tickets for the week despite the fact that he had a perfectly drivable car.

Malorie had assumed that all of the important British buildings that stored the remains of dead kings would be pretty centrally located in London, so she was astounded when the train ride took about 45 minutes.

Her father rambled on about why and how Henry was buried there. She figured he was at a point of spouting off any information he had pertaining to their adventure, but she could hardly keep her head in the conversation. Her sole focus was that they were one step closer to ending this thing once and for all and getting their lives back to normal.

Seeing the perfectly manicured lawn, bright blue skies, and stone arches made Malorie feel like she had just walked into Hogwarts. "This is a chapel?" Malorie asked incredulously. "It looks like a castle!" she tacked on, excitedly.

"Yes," her dad replied. "Windsor Castle, where the queen often stays, is on the other side of this plot of land. But to be fair, so many of these historical British buildings look like castles, even when they are not, so I can see why it would be confusing," Peter continued, chuckling at his own comment.

"Yeah, you're not kidding," Malorie exclaimed. "It feels like every new place we visit is just another set piece from the Harry Potter movies!"

"Too right, love," Peter replied.

When Malorie first arrived in London, she had found herself so irritated by all of her father's British phrases, yet now she found them kind of endearing. Shaking her head, she pondered, *What is happening to me? I can't believe this ghost queen is managing to bring us closer together. It feels like a betrayal to admit any warm feelings for him, but I'm having trouble maintaining the pretense.* She was so surprised to find her attitude towards her father changing that it was a minute before she realized he was still speaking to her.

"In fact, Henry was buried next to his third wife, Jane Seymour, here in 1547. He intended to have a fine tomb for himself complete with white marble pillars, gilded bronze angels, and life-size images of himself and Queen Jane, but his plans were not completed by the time of his death, so he was placed in what was meant to be a temporary vault for himself and Jane. In fact, we will walk over the plaque announcing his burial once we get inside the chapel," her father continued.

Malorie and her father stepped inside the chapel and Malorie couldn't stop her jaw from dropping. The tall white ceilings and white patterned marble floors, matched with stained glass windows lining the top halves of the entire structure, gave the room a bright and beautiful look to it. The place felt pure and sacred.

There was a hush that overtook the room. Malorie knew intrinsically that that was likely due to the lack of volume of people in the place, yet somehow the silence felt holy too.

There weren't many people inside, other than a priest or deacon or some sort of religious guy wearing a religious robe in one corner of the room. She supposed they lucked out coming here on a Monday afternoon, considering many people were likely at work at the moment.

"Can I help you?" the guy in the corner asked.

"No, we've found just what we needed, thanks," her father answered, pointing down towards the plaque.

"Ah, of course. We get many a visitor here to see where the famous Henry VIII and his dear wife, Queen Jane, were buried. I won't stop you. Carry on," he spoke and proceeded to wipe down objects Malorie assumed he'd be using for the next mass.

Malorie took slow steps towards the black marble slab on the floor, almost as if she were afraid if she got too close a phantom Henry would appear mere inches from her and scare her half to death. She cautiously drew close enough to the slab to read the words, "IN A VAULT BENEATH THIS MARBLE SLAB ARE DEPOSITED THE REMAINS OF JANE SEYMOUR QUEEN OF KING HENRY VIII 1537 KING HENRY VIII 1547 KING CHARLES I 1648 AND AN INFANT CHILD OF QUEEN ANNE." She didn't even bother asking her father about King Charles I or the infant child as she didn't care nearly enough and that's not what they were here for. But seeing Henry's name etched in gold made her feel *just* how real this was. His bones and dust were underneath the soles of her sneakers. The man who had tormented the woman attached to the necklace in her pocket was as close as he could physically be to her in this moment (she wasn't counting the impending arrival of his spirit as something physical.)

Her father jolted her out of her inner musings when he mentioned, "Prince Harry and Meghan Markle were actually married in this chapel and walked right over this plaque! Isn't that fascinating?"

He knew her answer would be yes considering that one of the many things he'd learned about her over the course of the week was that she was obsessed with pop culture, but she still felt she owed him the courtesy of answering so she said, "Yes."

"And the Queen attends Mass here quite often," he continued.

At that moment the priest left the room carrying his newly polished items and Malorie noted that she and her father were the only two people in the room. "Well, no better time than now to bring Anne into the mix," she remarked as she lifted the necklace from her pocket.

The lighting in the chapel was dim yet somehow the pearls still seemed to glow, possibly with Anne's phantom energy. Even the golden B of the necklace glinted in the dull light and Malorie couldn't help but note that she was holding something powerful and ethereal. Her breath hitched in this moment of awe and wonder, and she couldn't help but be grateful to be a part of this experience.

She held the necklace out to her father so they could both place a finger upon it and as they did, Anne materialized in a swirl of mist, just as they expected her to.

Her ghostly presence did not even acknowledge being brought back into their midst. Instead, she immediately crouched down and attempted to trace her fingers along the gold lettering that made up Henry's name. Of course, her phantom limbs merely passed right through, but it was clear seeing his name etched into the marble brought up many feelings for her.

She glanced above her once beloved's name to read Jane Seymour's name and the look she gave could have made venom curdle. *Of course, he'd chosen to lay beside this whore for all eternity,* she sneered. *He chose her in life o'er me and he chose her in death too it seems.*

At that moment, she glanced up to stare at the stained-glass windows. If Malorie and her dad were mind readers, they would have known that in that moment Anne was thinking about how Henry had brought her to Windsor Castle to make her Marquess of Pembroke. He raised her so high just to take her so low in the end. *It was hard to believe that such sweet memories could be mixed in with the sour,* she contemplated as she glanced down at Henry's name again, calling to her like a beacon. The gold lettering seemed to be saying, "Touch me. I'm here. I'm waiting for you!"

How doth we summon him? Anne asked brusquely, ready to stop reminiscing and get to business. She stood up straight and fixed her intense, dark eyes on Peter and Malorie with a mean glare, letting them know just how serious she was.

Malorie answered, "Well, you appeared to me when I touched your necklace. Perhaps we have to physically touch this object to make him appear too?"

"It's worth a shot," her father answered before bending down and placing his fingers on Henry's name just as Anne had moments before.

Nothing happened. Peter and Anne shared the same glum expression over the lack of activity, but nobody was willing to give up hope just yet.

"Let's try the necklace!" Malorie exclaimed excitedly. She gingerly placed the necklace on top of Henry's name, careful not to break physical contact with it so as not to lose Anne. She closed her eyes, ready to feel that rush of air and the coldness seep over her as it had done every time Anne was summoned, but nothing happened. She opened her eyes to see nothing but an empty chapel, her father, and Anne's pearlescent form.

As disappointed as she was that Henry still hadn't appeared to them, she had to admit that she was grateful that the chapel was still empty. If anyone saw Malorie and her father placing a necklace on a grave and looking around like they expected something to happen, they'd think the two of them were certifiably insane!

"Dad, Anne, do you see anything?" she asked, a little desperate as she was starting to feel excitement and adrenaline over this impending confrontation.

They both answered in the negative. Malorie was beyond puzzled. She was so very sure that would work. But she couldn't dwell on the disappointment too long, there was still a mystery to solve after all.

"Okaaay, so, what's our plan B?" Malorie and her dad asked each other at the same time. Anne managed to shrug her ghostly shoulders. *Back to the drawing board I guess,* Malorie mused to herself.

CHAPTER NINE

September 1533

Anne's throat was raw from screaming. Her sweat slicked fingers gripped her ladies' hands as she pushed and pushed with all of her might. This child had been torturous to carry and torturous to bring into this world but finally she was doing just that, bringing her baby boy into this world.

The windows in her chamber had long been boarded up as she awaited the arrival of the babe, but she remembered the feel of the crisp breeze of fall on her skin and she knew the river Thames flowed by outside. She couldn't wait to take her son for strolls along the river, enjoying the sound of the water lapping against the boats despite the stench.

Daydreams of her son had consumed her as she endured her lying in, but now her thoughts were filled with the agony currently affecting her.

"One more push, Anne," the midwife announced, and with one final effort, her baby was born.

She collapsed against the pillows, breathing heavily. Once she had regained some strength she asked, "What is it?"

Her ladies hesitated, fussing over the babe who had finally started crying.

"Answer me," she ordered, anger lacing her tone despite her absolute exhaustion.

"'Tis a girl, Your Grace," Lady Elizabeth announced apprehensively.

A wave of dread filled Anne's stomach and she was suddenly overcome with nausea that she knew had nothing to do with giving birth. This was just about the worst outcome she could have hoped for. She had made Henry so many promises for a son and now those promises appeared to be empty. Would he be angry with her? Disappointed? Afraid that he had wasted his time? Or happy that their baby girl was healthy and surely the next child, a son, would be healthy too! She couldn't predict Henry's reaction and that scared her more than she cared to admit.

She fretted over Henry's reaction, yet, to her ladies she remained composed. "Let me see her," Anne said, reaching her arms out for her daughter. "And inform the king at once," she added. She stumbled over her words a little because she did not truly want Henry to see this.

"Yes, Your Grace," Lady Margery answered and quickly scurried away.

Once the child was in her arms, all fears, doubts, and anxieties melted away for Anne. The child was beautiful, and Anne was in awe.

Her daughter wrapped her tiny fingers around Anne's own and Anne thought her heart might burst. Being queen, having Henry's love, none of that compared to the baby girl with her tiny cheek pressed against Anne's chest.

Anne hated that her first thought upon hearing the word "girl" come out of her ladies' mouths was dread because how could she ever feel anything but pure love and warmth for the baby girl presently snuggled against her?

The child had the wrong genitalia and deep, deep down this concerned her, but on the surface, she knew nothing but love. This child, this light of her life, this joy personified, was a part of her and she could never show hate or malice to the child despite the fact that she defied Anne's dreams. Anne had a new dream now, or rather, an additional dream. She still longed for a son, but this baby girl was a dream come true too.

"I will protect you always, dear one," Anne whispered as she kissed the top of her daughter's head. "I won't let any harm befall you," she announced as she stroked the soft faintly reddish hair that dotted her baby girl's head.

Henry thundered into the room, beaming wide, his eyes alight with pride.

"Where's my baby girl?" he asked as he reached for the girl in question. "Your papa loves you so much, do you know that?" he asked, holding her aloft as if to inspect her in the light. "And she's got my hair!" he announced incredulously, looking at Anne as if for confirmation of the tiny ginger hairs gracing their child's head.

So, he is not angry after all, Anne pondered and hoped the surprise did not show on her face. Truthfully, she was glad at Henry's excitement, it matched her own, but she couldn't deny that she feared his reaction would be a lot less positive. Did he love the child despite the genitalia she was born with? She hoped so but she feared she could not relax upon seeing the content look on his face because she had no choice but to try for a son as soon as possible.

"I thought we could name the child Elizabeth, after our mothers," Anne said, praying to God that Henry approved.

"'Tis wonderful!" he announced, eyes still glued to their child. Elizabeth cooed and Henry beamed so wide, Anne was sure she could see even the rotten teeth at the back of his mouth.

Anne let out a huge sigh and it felt like the first time she had breathed since Elizabeth had been conceived. She could never relax because she had to do everything in her power to deliver a healthy heir. Now the child was here so she breathed and sank into her pillow, eager to absorb some semblance of calm.

"Oh, but Anne," Henry started as he handed the child to one of Anne's ladies, "you have delivered a healthy girl and I am proud. I know a healthy girl means healthy sons are sure to follow. Come to my chamber as soon as you can, and we shall make a son." He kissed her on the forehead as he finished his statement and left her chamber without another word.

Dread filled Anne's stomach once more. A lot of responsibility laid on her shoulders and within her womb. She wished tiny, perfect Elizabeth could be enough. And though she was enough in Anne's heart, she knew she was not enough in Henry's mind. Anne could not let her guard down. She must keep striving for a son. It was the only way to secure her future and Henry's happiness.

Chapter Ten

August 2019

Malorie and her father looked at each other quizzically. Both were waging a silent war in their heads trying to figure out why their initial plans hadn't worked and if there was any solution they could come up with. A very scared part of Malorie's brain considered the possibility that Henry's ghost didn't exist, that his body and spirit had already passed to some sort of afterworld, and that since ghost Henry was not around there was no way for ghost Anne to finally receive closure and Malorie was just going to be haunted by an English Queen from the 1500s for the rest of her life!

She had a hard time believing Henry's ghost could have passed on to heaven considering all of the atrocious things he'd done, but who was she to judge? She wanted to believe in an afterlife as much as she wanted Henry's ghost to exist, and the two thoughts juxtaposed like that left her feeling like she was in a very weird position with all of this.

"Well, Henry's grave site was a dud, but maybe there's another grave we can visit?" Malorie asked, skeptical but hopeful. She pinched her chin between her fingers as she spoke and felt like she must look like one of those thinking emojis.

"Maybe you're on to something, Mal," Peter answered.

Again with the nickname, she thought. *Sheesh, when will he let up with that?*

Instead of voicing her thoughts, Malorie said, "What do you mean, dad?"

"Well, maybe *Henry's* isn't the grave to see. Maybe we need to visit the grave of someone who was important to them both. Maybe the connection lies in their blood creation, the union of the two of them," Peter said.

"Will you just get on with it and stop sounding so mystical and cryptic already?" Malorie sighed, exasperated, waving her hand as if shooing off an annoying gnat.

"Elizabeth. Maybe Elizabeth is the answer. Or, well, maybe her grave is at least," Peter answered. "Elizabeth I was the only living offspring of Anne Boleyn and King Henry VIII so it might make sense that her grave could hold some significance for Henry's spirit."

"Great! Let's go visit. And please tell me this place isn't like an hour away like St. George's chapel was or I might just take a walk outside into oncoming traffic," Malorie whined in an imploring manner. (Please note that Malorie had no *actual* intention of harming herself, she was just being as overly dramatic as possible.)

"Um, no, actually. It's just around the corner and we could walk there. To visit Elizabeth's grave, we must head to Westminster Abbey!" Peter finished with a flourish.

Malorie pulled her phone out to check the time. "Well, it's just after 1pm. We should have time to make a quick visit, right?" Malorie asked.

"I don't see why not!" Peter answered.

And with that, Malorie brushed her fingers against her pocket to make sure the necklace was still safe and secure, placed her cell phone in her other pocket, and walked out the door.

It should surprise no one that Malorie thought Westminster Abbey looked just like a fancy castle, although it still very much gave off church vibes as well. Which made sense since it was a church.

Yet something about the place haunted her too. It had a gothic feel and looked like gargoyles should be sitting atop it.

The structure had more spires than she could count, and tall, narrow windows loomed at her from all sides. Two tall towers stood imposingly on the front of the building, the left one graced with a flag that Malorie couldn't make out very well from this distance.

Malorie soon found that the inside was just as impressive as the outside. Black and white squares checkered the floor, just like at St. George's chapel. The most impressive feature was the stained-glass windows. From ceiling to floor on one very narrow wall sat large, arched windows with what appeared to be every color known to man.

There were also circular windows that reminded Malorie of honeycombs. They, too, had the most beautiful stained glass.

Malorie continued to gaze around in wonderment, noting the rich wood and plush, red velvet seats in the pews. Something niggled in the back of her mind that these seats were familiar, and she couldn't determine why. It took a few more minutes of determined thought before she came up with the answer: this is where Prince William and Kate Middleton were married!

"Wow, so we're hitting all of the royals' wedding sites, huh? Are you going to take me to where the Queen was married next?" Malorie asked jokingly.

"Actually, we don't have to travel for that. Queen Elizabeth II and Prince Philip were married here as well!" Peter said excitedly.

Malorie chuckled loudly at that, loudly enough that several passersby stared at her. Upon seeing the offended look in Peter's eye, Malorie clarified, "I'm sorry. I was only asking that rhetorically. But thanks for sharing."

Malorie looked from left to right, wondering where some royal tombs could possibly be stored in an area that looked like nothing more than a fancy church. She was just about to ask Peter when he said, "Come on. Let's go see Elizabeth."

He led Malorie into a side room with off-white walls and stone floors. The place had arches for days and a very interesting design to the walls with an endless pattern of rectangles and circles. It kind of reminded Malorie of the walls from *Harry Potter and the Chamber of Secrets* where there was a message written in blood. *Enemies of the heir, beware* and all that nonsense.

They walked up to a monument the likes of which Malorie had never seen before. Not only was it enclosed in what looked like a black wrought-iron fence adorned with golden baubles, but inside the fence were black columns with golden capitals. (That's the proper term for the tops of columns. You know, the curvy part that looks like something straight out of Greek architecture?)

Above the capitals was what looked like a bunch of family sigils. There were five, evenly spaced designs of crosses and x's all shaped like the old timey shields' men carried into battle with their swords. *Goodness, I should probably stop watching so much Game of Thrones,* Malorie thought to herself, shaking her head.

Above the capitals was a plaque written in gold on a black border. Malorie squinted up at it, and it took her a moment to realize that she couldn't read it because it was written in Latin. She went to take a step closer just to get a better view and see if any words stood out to her when Peter grabbed her arm and nearly shouted, "Stop!" She looked at him in utter confusion before realizing he was pointing towards the floor. Her eyes traveled to where she had nearly placed her foot and she saw a plaque that read, "NEAR THE TOMB OF MARY AND ELIZABETH REMEMBER BEFORE GOD ALL THOSE WHO DIVIDED AT THE REFORMATION BY DIFFERENT CONVICTIONS LAID DOWN THEIR LIVES FOR CHRIST AND CONSCIENCE' SAKE."

Malorie hadn't even had a chance to look at the likeness of Elizabeth, laying there in white marble, so entranced was she by all of the black and gold fanciness encasing her. But the plaque took Malorie by surprise. "Wait. Why does this say the tomb of Mary and Elizabeth?" Malorie asked her father, eyebrows scrunched in confusion.

"Because, as much as neither sister would have liked it very much, they were buried together," Peter answered. "See those black plaques, side by side, underneath Elizabeth's likeness?" Peter asked

Malorie nodded in confirmation,

"Those say, in Latin, 'Partners in throne and grave, here we sleep Elizabeth and Mary, sisters in [the] hope of the Resurrection,'" Peter said, pointing as he did so.

"But why were they buried together? Didn't they hate each other?" Malorie asked.

"Yes. Mary had Elizabeth imprisoned for most of her early life. Mary's tomb was actually placed here first, as she died first. Elizabeth's marble monument was placed above her later by King James I. Elizabeth was actually first buried in a wooden coffin in the vault of her grandfather, King Henry VII. She was placed here at a later date," Peter said.

Malorie began to circle the fencing around the tomb and as she did so, she noticed golden 'ER's' etched intermittently. *Must be Elizabeth's initials,* Malorie mused.

As she walked to the side of the monument, she was finally able to take in all of Elizabeth's features. Malorie stepped as close as she could and was able to see that Elizabeth's marble head rested on two marble, tasseled pillows. Malorie could see the way her nose hooked and just how heavily hooded her eyes were. Her lips were set into a grim expression and Malorie wondered if she had been this austere in life. A large forehead was topped by marble curls and on top of *that* sat a crown of gold and red with jeweled arches. Elizabeth wore a ruff around her neck that could have made Shakespeare jealous, and she was bedecked in many jewels. She wore a cloak that Malorie believed was trimmed with ermine. In one hand she held a scepter and in the other she held an orb. Malorie was pretty sure those were standard coronation accessories, cloak included. Malorie was in awe of this marble woman's presence and had no trouble imagining her to be a badass queen ruling England forever.

"Well, shall we take out the necklace now?" Peter asked.

Malorie glanced around to make sure no passersby were eavesdropping just in case more than one ghost *did* appear. When the coast was clear she produced the necklace from her pocket and unwrapped the purple handkerchief. Anne appeared in her usual swirl of shivering mist.

It seemed like her eyes were fine-tuned to hone in on Mary's name upon her daughter's tomb because the first thing she said was, ***How dare that wench lay beside mine own daughter in death!*** She attempted to spit on Mary's name saying, ***Bah! I curse thee!***

"Anne please. We don't have time for that," Malorie whisper-shouted (she was trying to keep relatively quiet so as to not bring unwanted attention to the pair of them). As she said this, she instinctively reached her hand out as if to grab Anne's arm and pull her back. It felt like her hand was sent through a bucket of ice-cold water. Her hand disappeared behind a haze of opaque fog for a fraction of a second before she recovered herself and pulled away. She shook it off and recovered long enough to say, "We need to see if touching your necklace to Elizabeth's tomb will bring Henry to you."

As soon as Malorie uttered the name 'Elizabeth', Anne seemed to realize just where she was. All thoughts of Mary were gone and instead her ghostly form quickly flew through the fencing so she could place a hand on either side of Elizabeth's face and whisper, ***My Elizabeth. My dear.***

Of course, her hands couldn't really touch the cool marble, but it wasn't for lack of trying. Malorie thought she saw pearly tears streaming down Anne's face as she continued attempting to stroke her daughter's cheeks, her curls, any part of her.

She grew into such a handsome woman, Anne said. Malorie couldn't quite agree with that statement, but she wasn't going to voice that out loud. ***She has mine own eyes,*** Anne continued. Now *that* Malorie could agree with. Both women had such intense, dark expressions in their eyes.

Malorie realized there was no way she would be able to reach the marble statue of Elizabeth as it was fenced in. She turned to Peter asking, "Do you think if I touch the necklace to one of those columns or something, it will work?"

"We won't know until we try," he answered, his eyes darting this way and that, trying to locate Anne which he would never be able to do as he wasn't currently in possession of the necklace. He continued, "The columns are connected to the marble slab that the marble Elizabeth is resting on so it should do the trick!"

Anne's pearly hand remained glued to Elizabeth's cheek. She still had tears in her eyes, but Malorie couldn't tell if they were happy or sad tears. It seemed like it would be easy to have mixed feelings about a child you simultaneously loved for being your own flesh and blood but despised for not being born with a penis. She figured Anne must be so overcome with emotion to be seeing her daughter as an adult, something she wished she could have seen in life but never got the chance. Anne looked on Elizabeth's face with such love and adoration that a part of Malorie thought, *Well, even if this doesn't bring Henry to us, at least she got to see her daughter fully grown.* The love she had for Elizabeth made Malorie smile as she thought of the love she had for her *own* mother, a love she was sure was the purest of loves and could not be replicated.

"Well, it's now or never," Malorie said. She looked around once more to make sure that she and Peter remained alone before pressing the palm that held the necklace against the cool, smooth pillar.

71

She closed her eyes in anticipation, but she didn't feel another blast of air and no goosebumps alerted her to another otherworldly presence. She knew before she opened her eyes that Henry wasn't here.

When she *did* open her eyes, Peter was looking at her with anticipation. All she said was, "He's not here. Let's go home."

Peter's lip trembled and he looked like he might cry but he quickly composed himself, his face turning stoic once more. "Too right you are, love. Let's go home and think up another plan for Anne," he said.

Malorie turned to Anne at that moment and said, "I'm sorry. We *will* figure this out. I promise," before wrapping the necklace in the handkerchief yet again and placing it in her pocket. Once the necklace was secure, she took Peter's hand and walked out of Westminster Abbey.

CHAPTER ELEVEN

Malorie was *beyond* grateful when Peter asked if she wanted to get food. He mentioned that there was a Shake Shack about a 15-minute walk from here and Malorie's mouth instantly started watering at the thought of digging into all of that meat and cheese. It was late afternoon, after all, and Malorie hadn't had anything to eat since the pancakes from early morning. "It's out of the way from the flat, but I figure we deserve a little treat after a bit of a disappointing day," he said with a smile. Malorie couldn't help but agree.

They ordered their burgers and fries to go so that they could mull over what to do next in the privacy of Peter's flat. They didn't need anyone at Shake Shack overhearing them talk about long dead kings and queens and calling the police on them!

As they sat at the kitchen table once more, munching on burgers, Peter said, "Okay, let's backtrack a little here. We never made it to St. Peter's Chapel in the Tower of London. That's where Anne was actually buried. It was the last stop on our tour, but Anne came to you beforehand, so we left before that final stop of the tour." Peter's brows were knit as though he were trying to solve a really complicated math problem as he said this.

"That's true! I hadn't thought of that," Malorie said, rubbing her jaw while lost in thought.

She had just reached her epiphany moment and she could have shouted with glee for how excited she was about it. She felt like one more piece of the puzzle was solved, and they were that much closer to sliding the last piece of the puzzle into place.

"Anne came to me when I touched the necklace. We've already determined that her spirit is attached to this object but perhaps Henry's spirit is attached to some object of relevance too! Perhaps his grave is not the container for his spirit just like Anne's grave was clearly not the container for hers!" Malorie explained.

Her father's look of determination was replaced by a look of disappointment, and she couldn't help asking, "What's wrong?"

"The problem is," he answered, "Henry was known to have thousands of jewels, furs, musical instruments, and books that were practically sacred to him, and many of those items still exist to this day! It could take us ages to figure out which item summons him. There are so many portraits, writings, furnishings, and more that can be found all over England! I don't even know where we'd start!"

"Well, we have to start somewhere!" Malorie countered. "What did he love most? Other than the women he kept tossing aside," Malorie said as she chuckled to herself. What? She couldn't help that her humor was a little dark. She continued, "Did he have any hobbies? Play any instruments?" She barely got the last word out when Peter cut her off.

"Mal, you're a genius!" Peter exclaimed as he grabbed her face in his hands and kissed her hard on the forehead. She was so stunned and taken aback, she didn't even have time to remind him how much she hated that nickname or to ask what the hell that was about before he launched into his realization. "He loved music! He played many instruments and composed many pieces himself. I think I know the perfect place to go that will connect us to his music," he declared.

He stood up and reached for his coat, hanging on the back of the kitchen chair. It was at this moment that he looked out the kitchen window and noticed where the sun was in the sky. It was far from setting as they were still in the middle of summer, but it was far enough along that Peter guessed it to be late afternoon.

He looked at his watch and muttered to himself, "It's about 16:30 now. The library closes at 20:00. We should have plenty of time even if we take a 30-minute ride on the train."

"Is there any chance we could *not* take the train this time? I know you love everything London has to offer but it's always so crowded and smelly. Not to mention usually cold and damp from all of this awful rain!"

Malorie said. She didn't mean to blow up on her father. In fact, they had been getting along a lot more lately. But she was so sick of acquiescing, and she just had to say her piece. Still having a little steam left to blow off, she uttered, "Not to mention you have a car we could be using, for Pete's sake!"

Peter was taken aback by her outburst. He wasn't surprised to hear it from her, they had been butting heads all week after all, but surprised that it took him this long to realize that this was her first outburst in a long while. They had been getting along so swimmingly for the past day or so that he had almost forgotten their relationship had started on rocky ground.

"I'm sorry, love. The train is the best way right now. The car needs petrol for one. And two, the traffic at this time would make it take ages for us to get there!" he said.

He wanted to appease her though and thought a compromise was in order. "Next time we need to go out, we can take the car. How does that sound?" he asked.

"Fine," she mumbled. It wasn't worth fighting about right now anyway. He had a point. She didn't feel such a strong urge to fight with him very much anymore anyway.

Malorie couldn't stop herself from groaning as she was forced to endure another long train ride. Although there was a semblance of peace brewing between her and her father, she was still a little disgruntled that she hadn't gotten her way and was forced into a situation she was not exactly comfortable with. Thankfully it was Monday, so it seemed like the train had a minimal selection of weirdos aboard today. Despite that fact, she felt discontented. They had traveled almost an hour to be met with nothing but some fingerprints on an old grave. Then they visited another location, fortunately very close, only to be met with nothing. Now they had to travel another half hour and Malorie wasn't sure what they would face on the other side. Either way, she didn't think she could face more disappointment.

They pulled up to the most modern-looking building Malorie had seen so far. She had been starting to think that England was nothing more than fancy buildings that looked like castles until she saw the British Library. The red brick exterior and the tiered layers of windows made her feel like she was on a college campus or something! Not that she knew much about college from personal experience, she was only sixteen after all, but she had visited her boyfriend Robbie, at college a time or two, so she knew how fancy they looked.

She sighed in despair. Now that she had let her mind wander to Robbie and those college visits, she couldn't help but feel her heart constrict with grief all over again. She hadn't seen him in a month even though it was currently a summer holiday because he was busy with some engineering program. He hadn't called all week and almost every time she called, it went straight to voicemail. When he *did* answer, he showed almost no interest in their conversation. Still, she tried. She texted him often, relaying all of the adventures and griping about how annoying her dad was but she was lucky if she got even a few sentences as a response.

She couldn't fathom why his behavior had changed. Just a few months ago, he couldn't get enough of her. He texted every night, waited for her by her locker, even had flowers sent to her home, something she'd never heard of a high school boy doing for his girl. She had felt cherished, and he'd made her think it would last forever. He told her it would.

Shaking her head to clear thoughts of Robbie from her mind, they walked inside. She soon found that the interior was as impressive as the exterior. Large white columns and endless glass made her eyes widen in awe. This didn't look like the type of place to house history, but she trusted her dad knew what he was doing.

He led her up many flights of stairs and through many hallways, showing his fancy historian badge to several people before they arrived at their final destination.

"Aha!" Peter proclaimed. "Here we are." He drew the last few words out as his eyes scanned the shelves. Quickly, he pulled out very old, very yellow, and very fragile looking paper secured in some sort of protective covering.

"This manuscript is referred to as Henry VIII's songbook. It is believed to have been compiled around 1518 and contains 20 songs and 13 instrumental pieces," Peter stated quite matter-of-factly, and Malorie was blown away that she was actually impressed by his historical knowledge for once. Alright, who was she kidding, she had been pretty impressed by his historical knowledge ever since this Anne adventure had started.

"Alright, let's pop that bad boy out of its case and meet ourselves a king!" Malorie said, a little too loudly as she was starting to draw glares from library patrons a few rows over.

Peter gave her a reprimanding look and then gently pulled the sheaf of papers from their protective covering. Malorie could tell by the way his eyes flashed from hope to disappointment that this was not the artifact to summon King Henry VIII from the dead. His hair didn't blow away from his face and his eyes didn't glaze over in awe so, as cool as this artifact was, it didn't have Henry's soul attached to it.

Peter said nothing, just shook his head very slightly, eyes downcast. Malorie knew better than to comment or make a smart remark as she was wont to do when she didn't know how else to handle a situation. Like she said before, dark humor was her go-to coping mechanism.

Peter was silent the whole train ride home. Granted it was only thirty minutes, but it was the longest thirty minutes of Malorie's life. And that was saying a lot, considering Malorie had once gotten her period in class and Teddy Hindelberg had noticed and decided to laugh at her until the end of class. She had to wait a whole thirty minutes before class was dismissed and she could go to the bathroom. It was the most embarrassing English class she had ever endured and had been the longest thirty minutes of her life, up until now.

It might have been the longest thirty minutes, but she was glad it was *only* thirty minutes considering how close Peter's home was to the library. Regardless, by the time they had arrived home, Malorie had decided she couldn't endure the silence any longer. They needed to think of a new game plan fast!

"Okay, so that was an utter letdown, but there have got to be some other avenues we can try to reach him. You said so yourself, there are other objects we can try. We can't just give up," Malorie pleaded. She knew her dad was still wallowing in their lack of success. Heck, she wanted to wallow too. A huge part of her couldn't understand why they were still persevering with this impossible task. What benefit was there for *her* if she helped Anne? She was just a young, American girl who seemed to have bitten off more than she could chew. But every time she thought about giving up, thoughts of Robbie swirled in her head, and she knew this wasn't just about Anne, it wasn't just about her, it was about every spurned love. It was about every love that went from sweet to sour. She knew it was too soon to call it quits and she needed to let Peter know too.

"You're right," Peter finally spoke. Malorie wasn't sure if she imagined it or not, but his voice almost sounded hoarse from lack of use.

"So, he loved music, right? What else did he love?" Malorie asked, trying to pry some answers from her father and encourage some next steps.

"Jousting!" he shouted almost before she had finished the question. "And I know just where we can find some joust-related objects!" He smiled at Malorie as he spoke. She was glad to see how quickly he had regained his pep and was ready to put his renewed energy into this adventure.

He began to pace the kitchen, stroking his chin all the while and clearly deep in thought as he continued, "But I doubt I can get us in on such short notice. Perhaps if I call Linda? No, it will still be too late. But I'll have to call Linda as soon as I can tomorrow. I'll need to pull all the stops and every high authority card imaginable if I want to get us in within the week."

"Dad, what is it? Where are we going?" Malorie shouted in order to pull Peter out of his musings.

"Oh, sorry, love. I lost track of myself there," he stated, pulling up short with his pacing. "Right, so I know where we can find some of Henry's jousting equipment and hopefully that brings him to us."

"Where, dad, where? You're killing me here, keeping this so top secret," Malorie said.

That smile returned to Peter's face along with a wicked gleam in his eye and - was she just imagining it or was there an apologetic grimace on his face too? "So, unfortunately, we'll have to backtrack a little. Remember how I mentioned that Windsor Castle is attached to St. George's Chapel? Well, we visited the Chapel but not the castle itself. And now we have to go back to visit the castle itself."

Malorie let out the longest, loudest groan an angsty teenager could possibly muster. "Come on, seriously?!" Malorie asked in disbelief.

"I'm sorry, love. I hope you're not tired of tours just yet," Peter pleaded. He *did* sound genuinely apologetic, but she had to put her foot down. They *had* been on one too many tours and he knew it because she had expressly told him so.

"Nuh uh. Nope. Not gonna happen," she stated emphatically, shaking her head all the while. "I told you I was done with tours," she very nearly shouted.

"Well, how about if I treat you to ice cream afterwards?" he asked, with a waggle of his brows.

She complained some more, arms crossed, eyebrows creased in fury, but finally she relented. "All right," she sighed. "I guess we're going to Windsor Castle tomorrow," she muttered with as much enthusiasm as she could muster. "Yay," she added her tone dripping with sarcasm, just to drive the point home that she was absolutely sick of tourism by now.

CHAPTER TWELVE

Malorie was tired of tours at this point, but she didn't have the heart to tell Peter that. Well, didn't have the heart to tell him *again*. She had already made her feelings well known. But, anyway, she would do anything to not feel the weight of the ghost in her pocket constantly anymore, even if it meant milling around with large crowds of people, staring up at mostly boring paintings and artifacts, and listening to boring know-it-alls speak in monotone voices about things she couldn't care less about.

She awoke Tuesday morning feeling glum again for the first time in a few days. Perhaps it was the fear that they'd only be further disappointed in their quest to find Henry's ghost, or perhaps it was the fact that missing her friends and family back home was really starting to weigh on her. And although she was dreading it, she was itching to get home and have the groundbreaking conversation she needed to have with Robbie once and for all. They needed to talk about why he was being so neglectful, and she needed to decide whether it was something she could keep putting up with or not.

Maybe she just had a case of the Tuesdays. Wait, did that actually apply to any day that was not Monday? Whatever it was, she put her game face on as she tied her hair in a ponytail and put on her sneakers. She needed to be able to face anything today, no matter how many boring paintings she had to look at.

"Mal, love, come to breakfast. Your oatmeal is ready!" her father shouted from the kitchen. She was glad they were finally getting along so well. Although still mildly unsettled by this developing relationship, she couldn't deny that being wary of him was taking more effort than just accepting the niceties he had been displaying for her. She didn't dread spending this day touring with him as she had the past few days and she figured she should show some gratitude for the slight improvement in their relationship.

She sat at the kitchen table, still bleary-eyed from having to wake up so darn early. Granted, tours of Windsor Castle didn't start until 10am and they were only facing a 15-minute commute to the place, so waking up early truly consisted of waking up at 9:30am, but what could she say? She was a sixteen-year-old girl on vacation, and she needed as much beauty sleep as she could get!

Her father had been up since dawn on the phone with his boss trying to get them booked for a last-minute tour. When he came into the room a few moments later bearing the largest grin she had seen yet, she knew he had succeeded where few likely could and she thanked her lucky stars yet again that her father was such a celebrated historian. There was no way they could have gotten so far on this quest to help Anne without his impeccable credentials.

"They're letting us in on the very first tour!" her father exclaimed. "Which means we have to leave in five minutes. Finish eating while I pack a few things," he said so fast Malorie could barely comprehend him. "Oh, and let's take the car this time. I think we've done enough train travel to fill our tourism quota, don't you?" Malorie breathed a sigh of relief. She was so tired of the stinky train and the weirdos that accompanied it. She was also glad that he was finally taking her feelings and opinions into consideration. This felt like a solid compromise since apparently, they had to continue with all of these history tours.

"Oh, and don't forget the necklace!" Peter shouted, his voice trailing off as he exited the room.

"Uh huh," Malorie muttered into her oatmeal. *As if I could forget the one object that changed my life forever and has got me running all over the dang country.*

Peter had warned her the night before that they'd be going back to the same location, but she couldn't help still feeling a little annoyed and run down. It was one thing to have to deal with tour after tour, touching object after object and receiving no results, but to have to keep journeying back and forth to the same places just added insult to injury. Thank goodness Peter had decided they could start traveling by car now. It was so much easier and more convenient. Even Peter, history buff that he was, seemed to be growing a little tired of tours after doing nothing else for a solid week.

Windsor Castle was exactly what she had expected in terms of British architecture, so Malorie had no trouble keeping her jaw firmly shut this time. It wasn't that she was tired of castles because she wasn't. She was just starting to feel like beautiful, ancient architecture didn't compare to having conversations with a ghost who now lived in your pocket.

But seriously, if the building didn't look like a location befitting a ballgown and tiara, then was it even really a British building? The gray stone, turrets, and perfectly manicured lawns would have made her jaw drop if she hadn't already seen so many jaw-dropping buildings during her time in the UK. She was halfway convinced someone from *Downton Abbey* might walk out at any second to greet her, so fancy was this castle.

Upon entering the castle, they were greeted by a chipper voice. It didn't match the plump, matronly woman that it was coming from, but who was Malorie to judge?

"Good morning! My name is Emma. I am here to assist in all of your needs during your stay at Windsor Castle. Are you here for a tour? The first tour will be departing by the left entrance over there in just a few moments," she said and gestured toward the entrance in question where a very bored-looking young man sat staring at his phone. Suddenly Malorie was grateful for her father's extensive historical knowledge because she'd be bored to tears if she had to listen to that guy drone on for an hour or more on all of the goods in this place. He looked like-and, she was willing to bet, sounded like-the teacher from *Ferris Bueller's Day Off* who calls "Bueller?" over and over again and gets no answer. She was tempted to go over and tell him that, but he looked like the last person in the world who would even know of that movie's existence.

"Um, no. We're not here for any traditional guided tours actually. My boss, Linda Chuthers, acquired special passes for us. We're just waiting for her and-ah, there she is now!" Peter explained, waving Linda over as he spoke.

A tall, smartly dressed woman with a pristine bob cut and gray streaks in her hair had just entered the building. She walked over to them and shook Peter's hand with a firm grip that suggested she had spent hours practicing it to be treated as the badass boss lady she was. She gave a curt nod to Malorie and the employee before stating, "I don't know what you need these for, and I don't want to ask. These will get you into any part of the castle should you require it. Please don't abuse this privilege or my head is on the line." She stated that last part in a tense whisper and Malorie had every certainty that she and her father could be heading into deep trouble if they didn't handle this quest with the utmost caution. As seriously as Malorie was taking all of this—Linda didn't sound like the type of lady you messed with after all—she couldn't help but marvel at how cool these passes looked. Black but lined in gold, on a silken lanyard, Malorie couldn't help but feel like she'd just been invited to meet the Queen herself!

"You know you can trust me, Linda," Peter said, giving her a quick, friendly pat on the shoulder before turning to Malorie and saying, "Shall we start?" He wanted to make this look like a legitimate tour so as not to draw any unwanted attention if it appeared they were starting to pay too much attention to any one particular object. Malorie nodded and with that they were off.

Peter was positively beaming with pride and excitement as they walked about the castle. He looked like he might bust at the seams if he couldn't dish to her about every artifact they passed and the historical relevance of it all. So, she let him ramble on. She figured it wouldn't be too different from the rest of the week and she chuckled to herself.

"Now, fortunately where we need to go is not too far from the main entrance. If you'll just follow me-" her father trailed off as he practically skipped down the hallway. Malorie was having a hard time just keeping up with him. Exhausted from the many tours they'd been doing all week, she was tempted to shout out to him, "Slow down!" They may be in a rush to reunite Anne with Henry, but that didn't mean they had to sprint through castle hallways!

The room he led her to was yet another eye-opening sight. Her widened eyes took in a circular, golden room with the tallest vaulted arches she'd ever seen. The way the arches splayed out reminded her of spider webs, but somehow it was a beautiful sight rather than something fearful. In the very middle of the ceiling was a gorgeous dome encircled with stained glass windows. It lit the room up but not overwhelmingly so.

Her father, who couldn't resist throwing in a little history lesson whenever he could, stated, "Here is where the Windsor Castle fire of 1992 started. If you look over there," he pointed with an index finger, "you'll see a stone plaque that commemorates the event. The restoration was a significant challenge that took about five years to complete."

"The room we are in right now is called the Lantern Lobby. If you're wondering how the room got its name, it used to be a chapel and these eight oak columns supported that vaulted ceiling as well as a central lantern." Peter gesticulated around the room as he spoke, and Malorie knew it would be clear to any average Joe just how much passion Peter had for this topic.

"But we're not here to talk about ceilings or lanterns. We're here to see this!" he said, flourishing his hand towards a suit of armor on the last word.

"If I were a betting woman, I'd say that since you told me Henry loved jousting and we are now standing in front of a suit of armor, that this probably belonged to King Henry VIII. Am I right?" Malorie asked with a smirk on her face.

"Too right you are, love!" Peter exclaimed. "Henry may have had an ulcerated leg in his later years, caused by a jousting accident, but in his younger years he participated in every joust he could. He would give tokens of his love to his first queen, Katherine of Aragon, and then Anne Boleyn when she took Katherine's place, before a match. It was suspected he had such a strong love for all things adventurous and athletic because his father kept him cooped up as a child, fearful he might perish, especially after the death of his older brother, Arthur."

"Wow, that's fascinating, dad. As much as I'd like to learn more, I feel like we should probably get this over with. Nothing for it but to touch the suit, right?" Malorie asked.

Peter nodded, but she could sense the hesitation in his posture. She felt the same trepidation. This was what they had hoped for, an object that tied Henry to this world and a chance to see him. But were either one of them really ready to meet him face to face?

"Well, here goes nothing!" Malorie said, and they both placed one finger on either side of the suit. They closed their eyes and braced themselves for the chill they got whenever they interacted with Anne. Malorie even looked down at her arm, hoping to see goosebumps for once, but saw nothing but freckles and hair.

"FU-!" Malorie shouted, but course-corrected mid-sentence and changed her shout to "FUDGE." That earned her a couple of stares from guests just now entering the lobby. "Sorry, lost an earring," she claimed, touching her bare earlobe, and trying to cover her tracks.

The guests continued on and as she looked back to Peter to ask, "Well now what do we do?" she noticed a tear shining on his cheek. She felt so bad. She knew she was beyond annoyed by this whole situation and felt more stressed than when she took finals a few months ago, but she had no idea the toll this was taking on Peter as well. She wasn't sure if it had to do with their so-far futile efforts to help or that he was merely disappointed he still hadn't gotten to meet one of his idols yet, but in that moment, she felt the need to reassure him.

"Peter, it's gonna be okay. I swear. We just need to come up with a plan C. Or is it D? It might actually be E at this point. We're going to find him though. I swear it," she proclaimed as she rested a hand on his shoulder in what she hoped was a comforting gesture. She never in a million years thought she'd be here comforting him rather than hating him but something about the journey they had been going on the past few days coupled with the conversations they'd had where they'd addressed his abandonment made her feel like they were truly coming to a resolution here. Maybe as mixed up as her feelings were- still hurting over not getting to know him for fourteen years, guilty because she felt that was partly her fault, and grateful because she was getting to know him now and it seemed like he was trying with every fiber of his being to make up for lost time- she could make some semblance of a relationship work with him.

"Okay, so what else did he love? What other connections can we make between some objects and where his spirit might be? Do you have any other ideas?" Malorie asked.

Peter lifted his head, that gleam back in his eyes. "Actually, I do!" he answered emphatically. "And if I'm right, we can find that in this castle as well. Let's go!" he insisted before grabbing Malorie's hand and dragging her off on yet another leg of this journey.

CHAPTER THIRTEEN

"Elizabeth!" he exclaimed. "Why didn't I think of it before? It makes so much sense!"

"Um, what?" Malorie asked. "No, we're here for Henry, remember? HENRY!" she shouted, drawing out each syllable as if he were hard of hearing. He brought her out here, subjected her to another tour, and talked about Henry VIII non-stop just to switch gears and start referring to Elizabeth? She wondered if he had gotten knocked on his head and she hadn't even known it. And what Elizabeth was he talking about anyway? She assumed he meant Elizabeth I, daughter to Henry VIII and Anne Boleyn, but they had already gone down that road and ended up with nothing. But maybe he was still focusing on objects right now rather than tombs.

"Hello?" she questioned. She wanted to wave her hand in the air to get his attention, but he still had a firm grip on her arm, dragging her to god-knew-where in this castle. "Can you please tell me what's going on here? What are you talking about? What do you mean 'Elizabeth'?" Malorie asked.

"Oh, I'm so sorry, Mal," he stated and then stopped suddenly. Malorie, unprepared for a sudden stop, crashed right into him. They had stopped in what appeared to be a hallway. She hesitated to refer to it as such because it was far from narrow and was probably bigger than the entire square footage of her mom's home back in America. But she assumed it was a hallway because it stretched on endlessly. It was marked by large windows on one side and fine portraits on the other. The ceiling was the beautiful gold she'd seen in that lobby room and the carpets were the most vibrant shade of red she had ever seen.

Her father pulled her back to the present when he continued, "My mind was going a mile a minute. But I've just come up with another brilliant idea!"

"Well, spill it!" Malorie insisted.

"We've been thinking of objects related to activities that Henry loved. But what if the object is related to a *person* he loved? And what if that person shared a connection to both Henry and Anne?" Peter quizzed, barely containing the excitement in his voice.

"Um… we already went down that road when we went to Elizabeth's tomb," Malorie said, eyebrows raised in a puzzled expression because she could not grasp why her dad was thinking of Elizabeth again when they had already explored that possibility.

"Maybe we've been going about this all wrong. We sought Elizabeth's tomb first, sure, but now that we're following the path of loved *objects* perhaps the object pertains to the symbol of Henry and Anne's love and union, their daughter, Elizabeth. Think about it, the necklace was given to Anne by Henry. There is an element of connection there on top of it being an object she loved," Peter said.

"Makes sense to me, and it's the only other plan we're working with right now. So, let's see if Elizabeth will bring Henry to us! Lead the way, dad!" Malorie exclaimed. The dregs of defeat were starting to dissipate, and she felt renewed and invigorated to have a new quest in the journey to chase.

They tried to walk slowly and calmly down the long, opulent halls and through the lavish rooms so as not to draw attention to themselves. There were many tourists here today, and it wouldn't do to have two people sprinting through the castle like they were on a mission. That would surely get them kicked out in no time.

Their final destination for this Elizabeth artifact appeared to be in what her dad had called "The King's Bedchamber." This room appeared to be just as opulent as the rest of the castle, although the walls were a bright red. That paired with a bed with golden posts and green and purple curtains-as well as a rug with swirls of green, blue, and purple-made Malorie think that people must have had some weird taste in the old days. She wondered why the royal family didn't hire an interior decorator or something. Probably so they could keep things as historically accurate as possible. She wanted to ask Peter about it but didn't think she could stand another long-winded rant about the importance of historical furniture and how 'interesting' it all was.

"There she is!" he pointed. His voice carried a little too loudly because at that moment he received at least a dozen dirty stares from tourists in the room. The wave of adrenaline that had accompanied his epiphany was wearing off and he suddenly noticed just how crowded The King's Bedchamber was. As the realization dawned, he realized he should have anticipated this. It was one of the most famous rooms in Windsor Castle and always had a large number of tourists crowded about. He realized they would never be able to converse with a ghost while tourists mulled around. He hadn't realized just how empty the Lantern Lobby was when they interacted with Henry's armor, but they were not receiving the same reprieve here. He was going to have to use his position of authority to clear the room before attempting any sort of conversation with Elizabeth's portrait.

"Oy! Everyone! I'm going to have to ask you to clear the room. I am a historian for the royal family, and I have important business here." As he said this, he flourished his badge. Okay, so he might have embellished the truth a little, but he *did* have the proper clearance here, even if he wasn't actually a royal family historian, and the badge proved he had valid credentials.

The crowd left in a huff, and he was sure he heard a few swears muttered under some people's breath, but at least he and Malorie had the room to themselves.

"Alright, now let's try that again, shall we, love?" Peter asked jokingly before saying, "There she is!" He pointed with a flourish to a painting of a young girl with ginger hair in a red and gold gown. Her face appeared solemn, and she held a book-Malorie would have guessed a Bible? -at her waist. The inscription below the painting read *Elizabeth I when a Princess c. 1546.*

Malorie didn't even have to hazard a guess as to who this was a painting of. From the portraits she had seen of Henry VIII thus far, she knew his ginger hair matched that of the girl in this portrait. And those dark, brooding eyes were an exact replica of the ghost that had been haunting her for the past few days: Elizabeth's mother, Anne Boleyn.

It was amazing to see the likeness of Elizabeth as a young girl when she had just seen Elizabeth in her old age yesterday. Yet it was easy to imagine that this beautiful, yet somber child could have turned into the woman with such a grimace etched on her marble face.

Malorie was afraid to touch the portrait, afraid to experience more disappointment if no ghost appeared. She never anticipated actually looking forward to feeling those goosebumps on her skin or looking into the depths of some dark yet translucent eyes, but she knew she needed this experience to happen in order to resolve the overall problem for Anne's sake.

"Well, here goes nothing," she sighed before pressing her palm to the edge of the ornate frame.

No chill brushed the hairs on her arms, no wind blew tendrils of hair from her forehead, and no ghost spoke some weird Shakespearean language she could barely understand. She was grateful that her father had made sure the room was clear because she could not stop herself from crumpling to the ground and sobbing. Peter held her as sobs continued to rack her body.

"It's okay, love. We'll figure this out. I promise," he whispered as he tucked loose strands of hair behind her ear.

Malorie couldn't understand why she was reacting this way. Three days ago, she hadn't cared about the British monarchy from twenty years ago, let alone from *centuries* ago, and now she found herself rocking back and forth on the floor of Windsor Castle because a king from the 1500s had not appeared in front of her. What was her life coming to that she had actually been looking *forward* to seeing a ghost? What teenager in their right mind would say such a thing?

She supposed she had just been so determined to reach the last leg of this journey that facing yet another dead end made her heart feel like it was splitting in two. This was worse than when Robbie canceled a date with her at the last minute, on their anniversary of all days. (She was really starting to think that once she helped Anne ditch her mean lover, she'd have to do the same thing when she got home.)

Never mind that now. She knew there was only one answer for this depressing turn of events. They had no choice but to regroup at Peter's home, hopefully over a piping hot cup of tea, and decide their next steps. She could only hope that their journey remained centrally located in London. That, and she was really hoping they didn't have to journey back to Windsor Castle a third time. Touring a place once is fun, twice is a chore, but a third time? Now that's just torture.

She couldn't remain a blubbering heap on the floors of Windsor Castle. She knew she had to pick herself up, dust herself off, and resume the mission. She may only be sixteen and not have experienced too much hardship in her life, but if there was one thing her mom always taught her it was that you don't give up, even when the going gets tough. And besides, she knew she would never forgive herself if she left the UK without putting Anne's spirit to rest. For the sake of young love gone wrong everywhere and for the sake of her inquisitive mind she knew they had a mystery to keep trying to solve.

Her eyebrows drew together, and a look of determination crossed her face. She was just about to stand up and suggest they put their game faces on when Peter spoke up.

"Perhaps not all hope is lost," Peter said in a dreamy voice. He had a far-away look in his eye like he was lost in thought. "We could visit the Royal Library right here, in the castle!"

"There are thousands of records on every British royal you could possibly think of," he continued. "There must be something that could help us connect the dots and finally find Henry!"

CHAPTER FOURTEEN

"We must head to the north side of the Upper Ward," Peter stated matter-of-factly as he took Malorie's hand and led her in a power walk in the correct direction.

"Wait, Peter! Can you elaborate, please? You mentioned the Royal Library but why exactly are we going there?" Malorie asked, huffing after every other word. She was a little out of breath and surprised at how fast Peter could move when he was on a mission.

"The Royal Library contains more than 200,000 items. And not just books! There are manuscripts, music, medals, and coins in addition to countless other objects!" he exclaimed.

Malorie hardly had time to process this statement before they were stopping in front of a beautiful, ornate door. As they entered, a surly looking man with a large, bushy mustache held up a hand to stop them and asked, "Pardon me. What business do you have here?"

Peter took the gentleman aside and spoke in hushed tones. Malorie saw him pull something out of his pocket and imagined he was showing the man his credentials. There were a few more minutes of murmuring and several head nods and emphatic hand gestures made before Peter returned to Malorie's side and stated, "Alright, love, we have clearance to browse the shelves. But it's policy to have supervision so this lovely gentleman will be accompanying us."

Fortunately, although it was the man's duty to follow them, he still respected their boundaries and kept a slight distance from them as they began roaming the aisles.

The library was light and airy, and everything was made from a light-colored wood. Large broad windows filled one wall and let in an abundance of sunshine. The room felt academic as expected but also somehow magical and surreal. She wondered if this is what it felt like to study at Hogwarts.

Malorie didn't know where to begin. Her eyes wandered over dusty tome after dusty tome, and nothing stood out to her as a possible container for the secrets of Henry VIII's spirit's whereabouts.

Peter seemed to have other ideas as he had already pulled a couple of books off the shelves. His eyes scanned the text frantically in search of answers.

Malorie didn't feel she had much to offer in terms of getting this research done. Even if she had been able to avoid all of the sneezing that stirring up dusty books would cause, she still couldn't comprehend any of the words written on any of these pages. She still needed cliff notes when they studied Shakespeare in English class so there was no way she was going to be able to interpret any of the words penned by these centuries' old scholars.

Malorie leisurely strolled around the library and let her dad do the studying. Fortunately, the security guy assigned to supervise them was glued to her dad's side. He must have thought of her as an innocent kid and was willing to leave her alone. He wasn't wrong, she *was* an innocent kid, and she was glad he was leaving her alone.

As Malorie wandered, something caught her eye. On a far-off wall, she caught a flash of bright blue and orange and immediately walked towards it to investigate.

She didn't have to read the inscription below the glass case to know that this was Elizabeth I once again. Her tight curls and the austere expression in her dark eyes matched the marble tomb Malorie had viewed earlier. And the ruff she wore in the portrait was just as reminiscent of Shakespeare as the marble ruff had been. In fact, if not for the youthful glow to her skin and her rounded cheeks, this might have been an exact replica to marble Elizabeth on her deathbed.

Malorie felt a magnetic pull to touch the glass case the same way she had touched Anne Boleyn's name etched into the monument at the

Tower of London. It was an ethereal compulsion and completely out of her control.

Malorie stared and stared at the portrait, fingers slowly reaching toward the glass. Those dark, hooded eyes seemed to beckon to her, insisting they had answers that she needed to uncover. She must have been staring for longer than she realized because suddenly Peter was behind her saying, "Ah, you found another portrait of Elizabeth I, I see." He smiled congenially.

There were no books in his hand and Malorie wondered if his search had come to another dead end. As if answering her thoughts, he said, "Didn't have much luck here. Are you ready to go?"

Malorie answered hesitantly because the mustached man was still a few feet away, "Peter, is there any chance we could take this portrait out of the case?"

He was confused by her request, and it showed on his face. He asked, "Why, whatever for, love?"

"I don't know how to explain it, but something is compelling me to touch the portrait. I feel like there are answers here," Malorie answered. She was afraid he might make a fuss or say they had already used his badge as much as they could, and they really shouldn't ask for any more favors. She really couldn't put up with another fight with him especially when she *knew* she was right and *knew* this was something they needed to do to complete their mission.

Thankfully, her request brooked no arguments from Peter. He merely walked back to the mustached man and engaged in another hushed conversation. After a few minutes, the man unlocked the case, pulled some latex gloves out of his suit pocket, put them on, and gently placed the item on a wooden table a few feet away.

"Be careful. Peruse at your leisure. Please inform me when you are ready to return the item to its case," he said in a posh accent. He then turned and sat at the adjacent table. He picked up a book that was lying on the table and began reading, occasionally glancing up to let them know he still had his eye on them.

Peter sat down and gestured for Malorie to do the same. There was a look of absolute trust and certainty in his eyes. Every time Malorie looked into his eyes and saw that trust grow deeper, she felt their bond growing and she was powerless to stop it. She didn't even think she wanted to anymore and as much as that scared her, it also filled her with a sense of warmth and security.

He placed his hand on the table, as close to the portrait as he could get without actually touching it. He glanced pointedly from his hand to the security man and back to his hand and she instantly understood that he intended to discreetly touch the portrait miniature so as not to draw attention from the security man.

He seemed to want her to do the same, so she placed her hand on the table mere millimeters from the portrait.

Without having to say a word, they both took three deep, calming breaths, looked meaningfully into each other's eyes, and touched the portrait.

CHAPTER FIFTEEN

The look of determination that shone in Malorie and Peter's eyes turned to pure terror as they felt the hairs rise on the back of their necks. While fear was very much present there was also a sense of anticipation that seemed to crackle through the air. Peter's eyes seemed to gleam with delight as he prepared to turn and face the man he'd been studying for decades: Henry VIII.

They both gasped in surprise when the vibrant, red hair they'd expected to see was on top of a fierce looking woman rather than a strong, robust man. They attempted to cover their gasps up as coughs when they received a severe glare from the mustached man. This seemed to appease him as he went back to reading his book.

Malorie clenched her jaw so tight she thought it might crack. She wanted to scream but knew she couldn't cause a scene while they were being watched. Yet she would have known those eyes anywhere as they were the same dark eyes that had been haunting her for days. Elizabeth I's ghost stood mere inches from them, and they couldn't say a word or they'd risk looking completely unhinged.

As Elizabeth opened her mouth to say, **What-** they both pulled their hands away and she disappeared.

"What are we going to do?" they both hurriedly whispered to each other.

Peter whispered, "Okay, we need to talk to Elizabeth, but we can't do it with that bloke so close."

"I have an idea," Malorie stated with the utmost confidence. "Follow my lead." She gave Peter a cheeky wink as she sauntered over to where the mustached man was sitting.

"Um, excuse me, Sir?" she started. Her hand clenched her stomach, and she had a huge grimace on her face.

Malorie liked to think she was doing a decent acting job at the moment and internally whispered a quick word of thanks to her mother for forcing her to participate in every school play from the age of six onward.

"I'm sorry to bother you, but I'm really not feeling well. Is there any chance you could escort me to a ladies' room?" she asked, mustering as much politeness into her request as humanly possible.

"I'm sorry, young lady. I'm really not allowed to leave any guest unattended," he said.

He sounded sincere and Malorie was grateful because it would be that much easier to trick him.

"I'm sorry, Sir. I completely understand your duties. But please? This is really an emergency," she pleaded. "I'm having *girl problems,*" she whispered. As she said this, she grunted a little in pain and clenched her stomach a little tighter.

If there was any phrase that could instantly make a man do your bidding it was "girl problems." Malorie found that men never wanted to question what "girl problems" meant exactly and were always quick to come to a woman's aid when she mentioned "girl problems", otherwise they might be mistaken as discriminating. Malorie knew a man like this would have to relinquish his duty and help a girl in need, otherwise she could file a complaint and he could risk losing his job and/or reputation.

"Ah, of course! Right this way, madame," he said as he gestured in the direction of the bathrooms.

Malorie couldn't help but glance Peter's way and give him one more cheeky wink before she led their surveillance far, far away.

Peter waited until Malorie and the mustached man were well out of eyesight before making any moves. He glanced around the library and noted the closest people were likely 50 feet away and all had their senses deeply embedded in the books they were reading. Nobody was looking up let alone stealing a glance in Peter's direction.

Confident that he could safely have a conversation with Elizabeth, Peter took a deep breath and, once more, pressed his finger to the portrait miniature of her.

Elizabeth appeared in a swirl of mist once again. Her piercing eyes glanced down at him behind her hooked nose and Peter wasn't sure he'd have the courage to ask her anything! Had she always looked so intimidating? He'd never noticed such a profound glare in all of the pictures of her.

Who are you? And what business do you have with me? she asked. When he continued to stare at her wide-eyed as he tried to sputter out a response, she continued, ***Speak quickly! I do not have all day.***

The anger in her tone prompted Peter to finally speak. "I- I'm so sorry, Your Majesty. It's an absolute honor to speak with you. My name is Peter and I have some questions for you."

Elizabeth completely ignored Peter and asked, ***Why are you dressed as such? I have never seen this style.*** As she spoke, she attempted to touch his clothing. She jumped with fright when her hand went through his shoulder. Peter winced at the icy cold pain that appeared to follow ghost touches.

Fie! What is this? What has happened to me? Elizabeth screamed. Her ghostly hand trembled with horror as she realized she was not simply human anymore.

"I can explain!" Peter rushed to say, hoping to comfort her. "I know this is going to be a shock to you, but this is the year 2019 and you are a ghost!" He probably could have been a little less blunt with that explanation, but he figured it was best to just rip the Band-Aid off.

Elizabeth's brow crinkled in confusion. Always the logical woman, Peter supposed she was trying to find a logical way to explain her present circumstance to herself.

2019? she asked. She said the number like it was a foreign word that she couldn't wrap her tongue around. ***Alas, that explains your weird costume and these strange devices,*** she said, gesturing to the laptops stationed at the tables surrounding them. ***But why am I here?*** she asked.

She seemed to be taking this better than Anne so far, or, at least Peter assumed she was. He hadn't been there when Anne had first appeared to Malorie so he could only guess. She didn't seem frightened as Anne had and she seemed to have no trouble processing that she was hundreds of years in the future. She just seemed curious to know more about this world and more about why she had suddenly popped into existence.

"That's a good question," Peter answered. "And I don't have a great answer for it. My working theory is that your spirit will remain here until you solve whatever unfinished business that has tied you to this plane of existence."

"I didn't know I'd find you," Peter continued. "I've actually been searching for your father."

My father? Elizabeth repeated in utter astonishment.

"Yes, your father!" Peter exclaimed.

Why wouldst my father be found in this strange place? Elizabeth asked.

"This is going to sound utterly insane, but my daughter and I found your mother attached to this necklace." As he spoke, he reached into Malorie's jacket, which she fortunately left draped over the back of her chair before she left on her distraction mission, and pulled out the necklace in question, still concealed within the purple handkerchief. He unfolded the handkerchief to give Elizabeth a peak of the golden B and teardrop pearls.

Elizabeth reached forward to trace the B with her fingertips, a look of yearning present in her dark eyes. Unfortunately, her pearlescent fingers slipped right through the necklace.

What is the meaning of this? Why do you have my mother's possessions? And if her jewels brought her to you then why is she not here? Elizabeth asked. *I wish to see her. Bring her to me!* Elizabeth demanded.

Peter should have known Elizabeth would assess the situation with logic, make the connection between the necklace and her mother, and ultimately demand for her mother's presence. He wasn't sure if he should bring Anne out right now. He was afraid of the commotion their reunion might cause if he couldn't keep himself composed. Nevertheless, it would be beneficial to see if Elizabeth had any inklings on Henry's whereabouts.

And if she needed to see her mother before she spoke to him, then who was he to deny her?

Peter took a deep breath, still attempting some semblance of composure. Realizing it was now or never, he placed his finger to Anne's necklace and watched her appear in her usual swirl of mist.

Chapter Sixteen

The raw emotion prominent on Anne's face was almost more than Peter could bear. She'd shown such love and adoration to the silent, marble form of her daughter they had seen previously. Now that her daughter was here in front of her, able to blink and speak among other things, her love appeared to have increased tenfold.

My dear Elizabeth, Anne said. ***How I have longed to embrace you!***

Her ethereal form flew towards Elizabeth and placed a pale hand upon her cheek. She knew the connection was nowhere near as lovely as a flesh and bone reunion would have been but the fact that they could stand side by side and be at eye level was something Anne never predicted getting to see. Her daughter, her sweet, sweet Elizabeth was a woman now. And though they may be nothing more than spirits, the fact that she could now speak to her daughter woman to woman was so shocking to her that it took the air right out of her ghostly lungs.

Elizabeth looked at Anne with her brow furrowed. *Mother?* she asked.

She had hardly begun to process this strange place she was in and now her mother was before her? It made no sense.

She had only been three when she'd lost her mother, but she could remember clear as day the day her governess, Kat Ashley, had told her she'd never see her mother again. She'd been told her mother was an evil woman and justice was on her father's side when he'd held firm in executing Anne.

She'd never believed in her mother's guilt, although she was told endlessly that her mother was guilty and never to speak of her. Although her stepmothers came and went as she continued to grow, she never doubted that her mother was the true Queen of England and should have grown old by her side.

She'd kept her mother's portrait beside her own for all of her years and now she could see that very face staring back at her, tears streaming down her cheeks.

Mother? she asked again. *Forgive me, but I must be touched. How are you here? For all my years you were naught but a ghost. A spirit whose name we must never utter lest we incur father's wrath. How is it you come to stand before me?*

Anne attempted to step forward once more, to be as close to Elizabeth as possible, but Elizabeth stepped back in fright. It was amazing that she could adapt to being in the future so easily, but not to seeing her mother. The two impossibilities could simply not fit cohesively in her brain.

I do not have all of these answers, Anne started. *But Peter here-* She gestured to him as she spoke and seemed to stumble over his name, as if he was just as foreign of a concept to her as the year 2019- *suspects that our spirits exist here in this futuristic world because we have unfinished business that we need to solve before we can fully pass on into heaven. I did not want to believe my soul was condemned to purgatory, but I know no other truth.*

Peter chimed in at this point to say, "That's true!" Finger raised emphatically upon his exclamation, he seemed to be eager for resolution. Adrenaline coursed through his body as he sensed it was coming soon.

He continued, "We believe that your mother's unfinished business revolves around your father. We believe she must confront him in order to pass on. It might be a long shot but is there any chance you know of where we might be able to find his spirit?"

Suddenly Elizabeth's eyes gleamed with anger. *I have just learned I am naught but a spirit myself and you expect me to know where to find my father? Bah! I curse thee for thy stupidity!*

Why should I know of my father's whereabouts? He cared not a wink for me. I was not the male heir he sought so he cast me aside as soon as Edward did come along. My stepmothers treated me better than my father ever did. I care not at all where his spirit now resides, Elizabeth exclaimed. She seemed to gain steam as she spoke and by the end of her rant, she was panting with frustration and anger.

Before Peter could even apologize for bringing Henry up, Elizabeth continued, *And what of me? Am I meant to remain in spirit form? Am I cursed to this purgatory as well? Won't you help me pass to the other side? Mother?*

She asked all of this in quick succession and at the last, she gazed imploringly into Anne's eyes. It seemed her angry facade had finally cracked as a tear trickled down her cheek.

Anne seemed still to be processing Elizabeth's "cast aside" comment. She seethed with anger and her words came out in a clipped tone like she was trying to hold herself back when she said, *He cast you aside? Just like he did me?*

At this, Anne wrenched her hands from Elizabeth. She spun away, her skirts a swirl of gray mist, as she began pacing in an attempt to control her anger.

He promised he'd care for you, no matter what. No matter what happened to me, he said you were his flesh and blood, and he would cherish that bond. I should have known it was all LIES! As she spoke the last word, she attempted to swipe a sheaf of papers off of a table. Unfortunately, her hand went right through it so the mess she intended to cause never happened.

He cast Mary aside so easily. I was a fool to think he loved us enough to never repeat the act. Sadness entered her voice now as she spoke in a wistful whisper.

She glided towards Elizabeth again and attempted to grab her hands once more. A light shone in her eyes like she was filled with elation. She seemed to be having an epiphany.

My Elizabeth, my darling. I am so sorry. You say he cast you aside, but I know he is not the only one at fault. I blindly followed in his footsteps, believing the throne was more important than my own flesh and blood. She glanced away at this, her eyes filled with sorrow and regret.

I was afraid for my own fate when you were born female, and I let it overrule me. I never showed you the love you deserved, and I am sorry for that. I fear you spent your whole life believing I did not love you enough because of the parts you were born with but believe me, I have been told how you flourished in your reign, and I could not be more proud. You were smarter and fiercer than any man and I am incredibly proud of you.

As Anne spoke, Elizabeth broke into a smile for the first time in many, many years. As her mother spoke, her smile grew bigger and bigger.

A tingly sensation overcame her, spreading from the tip of her head to the tips of her toes. She looked down to see her hands slowly dissipating. She knew rationally she should feel fear to see her body disappearing before her eyes, but she was calm. She was content. She knew her business was handled.

WHERE IS SHE? Anne screamed. She fell to her knees as best as a ghost could and began sobbing. *My dear, Elizabeth. Where has she gone?* Anne asked between sobs.

"Um, I think she's passed on. I think her unfinished business has been solved," Peter said uncertainly. He took a few tentative steps towards Anne. His instinct was to put a hand on her shoulder to show some semblance of comfort, but he refrained, he didn't want his fingers to turn to icicles after all.

But, what could that business be? And why have I not passed on with my dear daughter? Anne asked these questions like Peter was some sort of ghost expert. He was merely speculating but his speculations seemed to be correct so far.

"I think she needed to hear that you were proud of her despite the fact that she didn't turn out to be the much-desired male heir. And I think you're still here because you still have unfinished business. I think, if anything, this further cements that we need to find Henry in order to solve your problem. I think closure with him, more than anything, will help you pass on," Peter said.

Anne still looked defeated. Likely she wasn't ready to say goodbye to her daughter. She had lost so much time with her daughter, and she didn't want to lose her again so soon. No matter how much she yearned to set things straight with Henry, she had never dreamed that she'd be reunited with her daughter. It was bittersweet to see her gone so soon. She knew she should be happy that Elizabeth had finally found her peace but all she wanted was to hold her one more time.

"Well, I suppose our business here is done," Peter said.

But what of Elizabeth? Anne asked. ***I was not ready to say goodbye.***
She held her hand out to the spot Elizabeth had disappeared from as if she
could will Elizabeth back into existence.

"I'm sorry, Your Majesty," Peter said somberly. "I believe she is well
and truly gone. Passed on from this world. I believe we have no choice but
to set things right between you and Henry so you can join her once more.
And to do that, we must continue on this journey and find Henry once
and for all. He's not here so we must continue onward."

As he finished speaking, he placed Anne's necklace inside the
handkerchief once more. "I'll see you later," he whispered before folding the
handkerchief over the fine jewelry and placing it back inside of Malorie's
jacket pocket.

"I suppose I should find Mal and let her know that this portion of
the mission is complete," Peter said. As soon as he spoke the words aloud,
Malorie appeared with the mustached man in tow. She continued to
grimace and clutch her stomach and Peter grinned at her acting skills.

"Peter, there you are," Malorie exclaimed. "Sorry it took me so long.
I was having girl troubles," she said. Peter didn't need to know that extra
information but assumed she was saying it more for the guard's benefit
and to keep up the pretense.

"No worries, love," Peter said. "I think we've got what we need. Would
you mind putting this away for us?" He gestured to the portrait miniature
as he faced the guard and asked him that question.

"Of course, sir. My pleasure," the mustached man said.

Peter and Malorie lingered long enough to see him pull another pair of
latex gloves on. And, with that, they exited the library and headed home.

Chapter Seventeen

Malorie was full of questions, and she didn't even know where to start. She figured she should start with the obvious.

"Sooo, what happened to Elizabeth?" she asked.

"Exactly what we had planned for Anne happened with Elizabeth. I thought I was going to have to give them both a spiel about how I couldn't take Elizabeth with us because I couldn't take her object out of the library, but it turned out to be unnecessary," Peter said.

"Tell me exactly what happened!" Malorie exclaimed. "Is it just like the movies? Did she turn into a ball of light? Was there a peaceful look on her face? There always seems to be a peaceful look on their faces. And what was said to cause that anyway?" Malorie asked in quick succession.

"Woah, slow down, kid!" Peter said. "I know you're excited, but I can only answer one question at a time. I'm only one man after all," he chuckled

"There was no ball of light, it was more like she slowly dissolved," Peter said.

"Ah, like a Thanos snap. I got it," Malorie interjected.

Peter looked at her with a confused expression on his face. Leave it to him to be the only person who didn't know about *The Avengers*. Malorie rolled her eyes at that.

Peter continued, "She did look peaceful, yeah, now that you mention it. And it was a heartwarming conversation they had, really. Anne said she was proud of Elizabeth, and I guess that's all Elizabeth needed to hear."

Peter smiled as he spoke, and his eyes welled with tears. Malorie supposed he was emotional, not just for getting to see the people he had studied most of his life, but to see them bond like a real family and find some love and resolution amongst themselves. She wondered if he longed for that between the two of them like she did. She was starting to feel like she didn't have to long for it any longer. That after fourteen years of unanswered letters and ignored phone calls, she was finally willing to let him in. It helped that he had told her his version of what had transpired between him and her mother and she was starting to believe him. His actions this past week and a half had not been the actions of a man intent on neglecting his daughter. And as conflicted as she felt about finally releasing all of the hate, she had held inside all of these years, she was starting to think that it was finally time to let go of it all. She was sixteen, practically an adult, and she could say with conviction that she was willing to give herself whole-heartedly to this fresh start with Peter. Hell, let's be real, she could call him dad now. He'd earned it and she was okay with that.

She cut her musings short when she asked, "And did she have news of Henry? Are we any closer to finding him?" Her excitement grew as she asked this. She had been so filled with disappointment at these last few dead ends and now her hope was renewed because Elizabeth might have had the answers!

"Sorry, love, but no. She didn't have anything nice to say about Henry. She asked why she should know his whereabouts when he was barely in her life?" Peter continued.

Malorie was so overcome with emotion at this sentence, it took all of her energy not to let out a huge sob. She felt like one with Elizabeth in that moment. She knew too well what it was like to have a father that was barely in her life. But she couldn't vent about that now. He knew what he did wrong. They had already been over it. And they had made their peace. No matter how tentative it had been at the start, it was growing into a strong bond and Malorie felt like the resentment had slowly been seeping out of her pores this past week and a half. Still, she knew how that hurt could last years and years, just like Elizabeth seemed to know. She hoped Elizabeth could find peace with her father somehow just as she had found peace with her mother.

She muttered, "Bummer," in response to Peter's answer and they spent the rest of the car ride home in silence.

It wasn't that it was very late by the time they got back to Peter's flat so much as it was that they were both mentally and emotionally exhausted from the disappointment that plagued them all day long. They had assumed this would be a simple search. After all, if you can accidentally stumble across a phantom queen or two, how hard could it be to stumble across a phantom king? Answer: very hard, apparently.

While still at Windsor Castle, Malorie's mind buzzed with all of the questions she could pose to Peter and the possibilities of future locations they could examine to find Henry. But by the time Peter parked the car, brainstorming at the kitchen table was the last thing on her mind. She felt she might never be able to function again if she didn't get a hot shower and her head on her pillow stat!

Peter bade her goodnight with the promise of pancakes in the morning, and it didn't take long for Malorie to settle into bed and ease herself into a peaceful slumber.

Chapter Eighteen

The soft glow of sunlight entered through Malorie's bedroom window, and she woke, grateful to be well-rested. A hint of disappointment niggled in her brain knowing that the reason she was well-rested was because Peter let her sleep in, and the reason Peter let her sleep in was because they had no places to explore so far today. Henry remained as elusive to them today as he had been yesterday.

The eagerness Malorie had felt last night to put on her thinking cap and solve this once and for all was entering her brain again as she got dressed. She had always been inquisitive as a child, wanting to play Nancy Drew and solve the neighborhood mysteries like who really *did* steal the cookies from the cookie jar, and she found that with the discovery of Anne's ghost, that old curiosity was rekindled. She was ready to put on her thinking cap, or should she say her deerstalker! And yes, that was a Sherlock Holmes reference for you, curious reader.

She entered the kitchen and found a freshly steaming plate of pancakes in front of her favorite seat at the table. Peter had even made them exactly as she liked, with half the batch chocolate chip and the other half blueberry. He was truly shaping up to be an excellent father and the fact that the thought could cross her mind and not make her want to barf showed just how much their relationship had developed over the past week and a half.

"Thanks for this," Malorie mumbled through a bite of delectable pancake as she gestured to the delicacy in front of her. She was glad she had some breakfast to fuel her brain. She knew she needed to have all gears turning this morning if they had any hope of solving the current mystery of Henry's location.

Peter sat across from her and slid a piping hot cup of coffee her way. *Smart move, dad,* she thought. In the next moment, he slid over a bottle of creamer and a small bowl of sugar. *Extra smart move, dad,* she thought. He remembered that she liked her coffee to taste as little like bitter bean water as possible, so she was very grateful for the opportunity to doctor up her beverage. He was already anticipating the hard work they were likely to go through this day and was arming them with extra caffeine. With that, they settled down to brainstorm yet again.

After about ten minutes of hard thought, in which she felt like her head must be smoking from how hard the gears were turning in her brain, she realized there had to be a sensible connection between which ghosts were attached to which objects.

Suddenly it hit her like a ton of bricks thrown at her chest. Maybe Anne's object, the necklace, had a connection to Henry. And if that were the case, maybe Henry's object would have a connection to Anne, and *just* Anne. She touched the necklace as she spoke as if it were the only talisman anchoring her to this moment. The touch was only brief as she wasn't quite ready to bring Anne into the brainstorming session just yet. Her head was already in enough turmoil without adding an angsty ghost to the mix.

"Dad, Henry gave Anne this necklace, right?" she asked, gesturing to the necklace.

"Of course Henry gave it to her," her father answered.

"Then maybe the object we need to find for Henry is one that connects him to Anne too. Not something they both loved or a person they both had a connection with but an object that she gifted to him, or he gifted to her out of love. Perhaps it would be even more significant if it was an object connected to the beginning of their courtship or to their wedding," Malorie stated.

Peter took her by surprise as he planted a huge kiss on her forehead, once more, much to her chagrin. "You're a genius, Mal! That must be it!" he exclaimed. Malorie grumbled a little at the use of the despised nickname, but his cheer was infectious, and she couldn't help smiling. Malorie could tell it was taking all of his effort not to jump with glee in the middle of his little kitchen.

"I can think of a couple of objects of Henry's that have ties to Anne," Peter said.

"So, what objects may connect them, dad? Items that still exist now, anyway," Malorie continued. Holy crap, what if the item didn't exist anymore? Then they would *never* find Henry and Anne would *never* get the closure she needed. Sure, Malorie wouldn't necessarily be *haunted* if she just didn't touch the necklace, but she feared a part of her would always yearn for Anne and Henry's reconnection. It would be like completing a puzzle but missing one final puzzle piece. It would never really feel finished. She was starting to get heart palpitations just at the thought.

Her father interrupted her panic by saying, "The first and most obvious thought that comes to mind is the love letters Henry wrote to Anne while he was courting her. Anne's replies were lost, but the letters Henry wrote to Anne live in the Vatican Library today. It was thought they might live there now because they were taken from her as Henry sought an annulment from Katherine of Aragon and those letters were the evidence the papacy was trying to use against Henry."

"Yup, that sounds like it could be a decent contender," Malorie responded as she took a sip of coffee. Always one for some semblance of organization, she opened the notes app in her phone and began typing "Vatican Library" under "List of places to look for Henry". She figured it couldn't hurt to try to maintain some order to the chaos of trying to track down a ghost. She continued, "But do you have any other ideas? It's probably best to keep our options open."

Peter thought for a moment before exclaiming, "Oh yes! There's the famous golden, ornate clock that Henry gifted to Anne in 1533 as a wedding present! It's engraved with the initial's 'H' and 'A', truly a most remarkable object signifying their union."

Malorie glanced down at her phone to add in this new information. "Well, you mentioned that the letters are in the Vatican Library, so all the way in Rome. Is this clock at least a little closer to home?" Malorie asked. As she did so, she opened a new tab in her phone where she could note the locations of the objects they intended to track down.

"Indeed. It's kept at Strawberry Hill House in Twickenham. It's just about 30 minutes from London by car," Peter answered.

Malorie added those locations to her phone then said, "Well, we clearly haven't managed to find him attached to objects tied to his hobbies or his daughter, so I think this is our next best option. Let's call it plan D.

Or are we on plan E already? I actually think we might be on plan F by now!" Her little joke made her chuckle to herself, and Peter let out a pity laugh in return.

"I agree," Peter declared.

"I think our next step has to be checking out these objects then. But they're in two different locations. Maybe we should split up?" Malorie suggested. "We don't know how many objects we might have to track down and it will likely take too long if we continue to go to each place together. Besides, we haven't had much luck traveling together and this is the first time that an object we seek is in another country all together. We've lucked out so far only seeking objects within a thirty-minute walk or subway ride of the flat but I'm only here until the end of the week so if we now have to plan a trip to Rome and back, we better make it quick," Malorie continued

"Right you are," Peter answered. He pulled his decrepit flip phone out and stared intently at the screen, brow furrowed in concentration.

"Don't tell me you're trying to buy a plane ticket from that ancient thing," Malorie managed to utter between guffaws.

"What? I'll have you know, this ancient thing has booked me plenty of tickets to places all around the world."

"Uh huh, sure, gramps. Try not to throw your back out while you hunch over that tiny screen. I'll be right back," she said as she swiftly left the room and returned with her sleek, state-of-the-art laptop. Of course she knew she could have ordered a plane ticket from her non-decrepit phone, but she liked the bigger screen that the laptop provided.

"Give me a sec," she muttered to herself. She did a lot of clicking and clacking on her laptop, asking Peter for his credit card and ID info a few times. "Annnnnd voila!" she exclaimed with one final click. "I should be receiving an email shortly with confirmation of my flight. I can't believe I managed to squeeze onto a flight leaving tomorrow morning so we won't have to waste a day! This flight leaves at 8am tomorrow from Heathrow."

"That's great news, Mal! You ought to pack a travel bag in case things at the Vatican take longer than anticipated and we can't get you home overnight," Peter said.

Malorie plopped her duffle on her bed and contemplated what to pack. She withdrew Anne's necklace from her pocket, still carefully wrapped in the handkerchief, and pulled back the material far enough to see the gleaming, golden B. She couldn't believe such a tiny, dainty thing could have caused her so much stress in the span of a few short days. Yet somehow, she was grateful to this necklace and to Anne for making Malorie feel alive for the first time in so long. (Yes, she saw the irony in a ghost making her feel alive. Very funny.)

Malorie hadn't realized she'd been longing for an adventure and that a piece of her soul was missing until she started this adventure. She hadn't realized that she missed solving mysteries like she used to do when she was a pre-teen and that having a new mystery to solve gave her a thrill like no high school boyfriend ever could. She was beginning to think fate brought her to London, not just to bring her and her dad together, but so she could find Anne and help her fulfill her destiny.

Malorie was tempted to let her skin graze one of the precious pearls in order to call Anne to her but thought better of it. As much as she enjoyed the purpose Anne gave her, she still wasn't entirely comfortable with all of the old timey language that she could hardly understand.

She replaced the necklace in her pocket and started placing toiletries in her bag, making sure to double- and triple-check that her passport was packed. Her mind was whirling with what they had already uncovered through Anne and the very real possibility of uncovering Henry in Rome or thirty minutes down the road in Twickenham. It blew her mind to think that there was the possibility that she'd be facing another phantom monarch very soon. She didn't know what she'd do when she met the ghost king. Does one still bow to dead royalty?

When she finally settled down for bed, she found herself quickly drifting off to sleep. Soon she found herself dreaming of ghost Henry kindly asking her to dance and then immediately demanding her beheading.

She woke abruptly, chest heaving and sweat dripping down her face. She glanced at the necklace again and thought there was some truth to the nightmare, and now she found herself equal parts terrified and apprehensive to meet Henry. She knew they had to find him soon, but she couldn't deny that a part of her dreaded the chance of finding him in Rome.

CHAPTER NINETEEN

She was tired of her days starting bright and early, yet here Malorie was *again*, waking up with the sun so she could catch her flight to Rome. *Holy crap! I'm going to Rome! Setting for The Lizzie McGuire Movie. Hehe, maybe I'll meet my Paulo there.* What? A girl could dream, couldn't she?

Despite the energy drain from the chaos of the morning, Malorie was invigorated with the thought of traveling to Rome. She walked into the kitchen, shocked to not be greeted by the delicious fragrance of pancakes, bacon, or even a single slice of toast. Instead of preparing her breakfast, Peter was busy packing last-minute things and muttering to himself. She walked over to him just in time to see him throw sunscreen in her bag, saying, "What? You can never be too careful."

"It has been nothing but cloudy this whole week and Rome is anticipating cloudy weather too," she retorted, showing him the weather app on her phone.

"Still, I'd like to make sure your skin is nice and safe," he responded.

She wanted to laugh, and a small part wanted to resent him still for his absence, but it was so hard when he showed how much he cared for her like this.

"Alright, love, we better get a move on. It's a thirty-minute drive to the airport," Peter said.

"Come on, dad! Hurry up!" Malorie whined, peaking around her father's shoulder as he stood in front of a kiosk in the airport terminal trying to print out her ticket to Rome.

"I'm going as fast as I can, Mal! But there's a lot of information to input," he said as his fingers continued to tap away.

"How could there possibly be more information to input? I already did it all online when I bought the ticket!" she almost shouted in her frustration.

"I dunno, love. I'm just doing what the machine says."

Malorie's duffle was small enough to count as a carry on, and she had tucked Anne's necklace carefully in a pair of socks and placed it toward the bottom of the bag last night. Malorie was still sweating bullets though, fearing they might take the real artifact away from her, and subsequently take Anne away too. The internal fear she was feeling translated to the huge wave of jitteriness she was portraying outwardly and explained why she couldn't stop pacing back and forth as her father continued to fiddle with the machine. She noticed her hands were shaking with her anticipation. She wondered why she felt so light-headed and realized it was because she forgot to breathe.

C'mon, Malorie. Breathe In…1…2…3…Out…1…2…3. You got this, she encouraged herself.

"There we go!" her father exclaimed just as the boarding pass printed.

There wasn't really a rhyme or reason as to why they decided Peter would go to Twickenham and Malorie would go to Rome other than Malorie wanted to fly and get to see more of the world and Peter didn't mind going for a bit of a drive in the English countryside. It helped that he had his own car and already had a very solid sense of the backward driving these Londoners called normal. Regardless, that was their decision and Malorie was taking Anne with her in a duffle bag.

Peter was surprisingly chill for a parent about to send his daughter off to another country. Malorie soon learned this was because his parents let him travel in his late teens too. They had insisted that he see the world and get as much cultural experience as he could. Now he wanted his daughter to have the same opportunities, especially since he hadn't been able to give them to her earlier in her life due to his own foolish mistake.

Peter further insisted that they not mention this to Malorie's mother which was just fine by her! His reasoning was that she was already stressed about Malorie staying a little longer overseas and they didn't want to give her any more reason to worry. Plus, a nagging mom calling every few minutes would *really* hinder the search process.

"Call me when you land!" her father insisted before giving her a kiss on the forehead and sending her off through the terminal. She couldn't know it, but he stood by the kiosk long past the time she made it through the terminal and to her gate. He couldn't help but fear. He had just reunited with his daughter, and he was afraid he might be sending her off to some sort of danger he couldn't protect her from on this trip to Italy.

Besides, if she really found Henry in Italy, there was no guaranteeing how volatile he might be. He could be just as destructive in death as he was in life, and Peter was afraid to think of what damage he might be capable of, even in his incorporeal form.

Malorie loved how close everything was in Europe! In the U.S., a two-and-a-half-hour flight would just get you from the top of one coast to the bottom of the same coast, but here in Europe all it took was a two-and-a-half-hour flight to get her from London to Rome. She hardly had time to put her earbuds in and really relax before the flight attendant was telling all passengers to place their seats and trays in the upright position and prepare for landing. Malorie took a deep breath, gathered her bag, and stepped off the plane for the next leg of her journey.

It occurred to Malorie as she walked through the airport and heard groups of people conversing in Italian that she didn't know a lick of Italian. She hoped she wouldn't have a hard time asking for directions to the Vatican despite her lack of knowledge of the language. Would her two years of basic Spanish in middle school at least help a little bit with the language barrier? Only time would tell.

As Malorie exited the airport, she realized the language barrier was not the only hurdle she'd have to jump through. She found it hard to ask for directions merely because people didn't want to give her directions. She didn't think any place was capable of having people as rude as the New

Yorkers she encountered on her visits to the city, but she soon found that Rome could give New York a run for its money. She couldn't count how many sleazy people she ran into who just wanted to hit on her or try to sell her things (No, she was not going to pay 10 euros for a flimsy selfie stick thank you very much!) before she found a kind, old lady who pointed her in the right direction.

"Grazie!" she shouted as she ran in the direction the lady pointed her in. She didn't have to know much Italian to know how to say thank you. It certainly helped that her mom told her what the word "grazie" meant one year when she asked after seeing it on the Olive Garden after-dinner mint wrapper.

As she ran toward the Vatican, she called her dad to let him know she'd arrived safely. She was huffing for air through the conversation as she ran through the streets of Rome but at least she got the job done.

When she arrived at the entrance to Vatican City, she was astounded to come face to face with a large imposing wall. She couldn't imagine how an important historical and religious institution could look so closed off from the rest of the world, but she supposed if it was holding artifacts such as Henry VIII's letters, it made sense to be a little closed off and cautious. Plus, since when have the Catholics been known to be super warm and inviting, right?

The line wasn't unbearably long, which was another godsend, and before she knew it, she was in.

She quickly found an English-speaking tourist who had just finished the full tour and was able to point her in the direction of the Vatican Library in no time. Luck was truly on her side. Or was it fate? Was she destined to meet Henry's ghost just so she could save the ghost of Anne Boleyn?

Malorie was never much of an art buff, but she wished she had more time to marvel at the infinite amount of paintings on the ceilings and walls. The room was brightly lit, and the pattern of the tile made it feel like she was in a palace. She never expected a religious institution to look so sumptuous.

Although Malorie found it easy enough to get into the Vatican as a whole, she soon realized it was going to be a lot harder to track down the letters than she realized, and she wasn't entirely sure anyone would allow a sixteen-year-old kid to see them even with the right credentials. Nevertheless, she had to try. And she had to hope and pray that her father's name would be enough to get her through this quest as it had done so before.

After asking around in broken Spanish and getting replies in broken English, she soon learned that the letters were kept in the Pope's private library. Many employees warned her she'd never be able to get in, but she insisted they point her in the right direction because she couldn't leave this place without trying.

She was instructed to pass through the Porta di S. Anna and was met by Swiss Guards who asked for photo ID and a letter of admission. "I'm here on behalf of my father, Peter Bennington. He's a historian for Oxford," Malorie said as she pulled out her passport.

"Where's your letter of approval?" the guard asked in heavily accented English as he glanced at her passport and handed it back.

"I don't think you heard me. My father is a world-renowned Tudor historian. He has been here before and he's allowed to be here again. I am here on his behalf," Malorie answered, anger tingeing her voice.

"I'm sorry, ma'am. No letter, no entry. I can't let you in today."

Malorie wanted to curse and scream and throw the largest temper tantrum imaginable, but she knew it would only be wasted on this man and wouldn't get her anywhere. Instead, she found the nearest bench and sat down to make a phone call to her dad.

"Why didn't you tell me I'd need some special letter to see Henry's letters, dad!? Now I'm stuck in Vatican City, but they won't let me into the building I need to be in. I should have just let you come to Rome. Curse me for wanting to be a world traveler," she grumbled.

"Oh, bollocks!" her father exclaimed. "I can't believe I forgot you'd need my documentation to get in! You're right. I should have just gone instead," he said, and she could tell he was laying his head in his hands as he said it just from how exasperated he sounded.

"How about this," he continued. "I'll email you the documents you need, you can print them out at a local library or some such and try all of this again. I know it's all a pain in the arse and I'm sorry, love. I'll have my company buy you another ticket for entry into the Vatican. Sound good?"

All Malorie could do was answer in the affirmative and try all of this again. She didn't care if she needed to kidnap the Pope himself to get herself into that room and find Henry VIII. She would do absolutely anything to help Anne and lay her spirit to rest once and for all. It wasn't just that helping Anne would feel like fitting that last puzzle piece into its properly fitted location, it was that helping Anne felt like she could finally help herself when it came to her *own* relationship. She thought if she could be brave enough to help Anne and Anne in turn could be brave enough to face Henry, then Malorie could be brave enough to confront Robbie once and for all about the state of their relationship and put an end to it if need be... and it was looking more and more like the need was *definitely* there.

A few hours later, Malorie found herself outside the same wrought iron gate the Swiss had turned her away from before. Armed with the proper paperwork and identification, which only took a whole lot of running around the city, pleading with officials, and trying not to burst into tears, Malorie was ready to face off with these guards and stand her ground. Fortunately, she didn't have to raise any fists or give any evil glares as they merely glanced at her paperwork and let her in this time around. Malorie had never found herself more elated to be so close to placing another piece of the puzzle smoothly into place.

After much ID scanning and being transported from one room to the next, Malorie was finally led to the Vatican Document Reading Room. The gold walls and white ceiling coupled with high arches made Malorie feel like she was sitting down to read in heaven. The room still screamed "library," but it was definitely the kind of library that she could see angels sitting at with a nice book or trying to tuck their wings in to avoid knocking any books off the shelves.

She was told to sit and wait for the documents to be brought to her. After all of the hassle and waiting she'd already been put through she didn't mind waiting another few minutes. But a few minutes turned into an hour before a librarian came out with old looking books on her cart.

Malorie handled the pages as gingerly as possible. Her fingers tingled like she'd stuck her hand in an electric fence and she realized it was the overwhelming sensation of knowing that she was touching paper that was nearly five hundred years old and had been touched by a king. It was almost too much to bear to realize just how closely she was engaging with history.

She scanned through the very first letter, finding phrases like "dart of love" and "a place in your heart and affection" and "I will go thither with all my heart" and she could finally fully grasp just how madly in love this man was with the spirit attached to the necklace still resting in her pocket.

She read another letter to find a passage where Henry wrote, "wishing myself (especially an evening) in my sweetheart's arms, whose pretty dukkys I trust shortly to kiss". She raised an eyebrow at this. *What the heck did "dukkys" mean?* she wondered. She discreetly pulled out her phone to google the term and her eyes widened when she learned "dukkys" meant breasts! Her hand flew to her mouth as she stifled a gasp. Henry was writing erotically to Anne she realized!

Men never change, she thought. *Ruler of England and head of his own church and still all he can think about is a woman's boobs.* She could only shake her head at this man's intentions as she set the letter aside. Still, this was something she never expected to read from a sixteenth century monarch's own hand.

Malorie had just gotten through reading the passage, "or what joy can be greater upon earth than to have the company of her who is dearest to me" and thinking how entirely sweet and infatuated this man was and how entirely implausible it seemed that he could write these things and then go about killing the woman he wrote them for, when she realized she was touching the flaky, fragile pages of nearly 500-year-old paper and Henry had not appeared to her yet.

That's strange, she thought. *Maybe I need to touch the necklace to the page. Maybe object-touching-object is how the magic happens.* She wasn't sure how she'd be able to discreetly pull the necklace out with the librarians watching, but she had to find a way to test out this theory. She continued to flip pages with one hand while pulling the handkerchief-wrapped necklace from her pocket with the other. She slipped the necklace up her sleeve and placed her arm on the table by the book. When the librarians turned their heads, she unwrapped one tiny pearl and placed the yellowing jewel against the yellowing page.

She closed her eyes in anticipation, expecting to feel the cool rush of air that always accompanied Anne's arrival. Nothing happened, no strands of hair out of place, no goosebumps, nothing.

She opened her eyes to see nothing but a librarian looking at her with a quizzical look in his eye. *Crap,* she thought. *Well, this was clearly a waste of time!*

Just as the thought sprang into her head, her cell phone buzzed. After receiving a glare that could have made hell freeze over—cell phones weren't allowed in the library and the stare the librarian was giving her made it clear she should have known this already—she ran out of the room to answer it. Seeing the call was from her father she answered instantly. Before she could even get two words out to tell him this adventure had been a bust, he said in a cryptic whisper, "He's here." ·

Chapter Twenty

Autumn 1526

"My dear Anne, a gift has arrived for you. A gift from the King!" her father announced, gasping for air as if he had run all the way to her chambers to tell her of this wondrous news. Thomas Boleyn was an intuitive man and as soon as he had noticed that the king had set eyes on his daughter, he was eager to see how high the king's affections might raise him and his family. After all, the whole court knew how the king had provided for his mistress, Elizabeth Blount, and the bastard boy she gave him, Henry Fitzroy, so what was to stop the Boleyn's from claiming such favors? Anne's attitude apparently.

"Put it away, Father. I have no mind to see what sweet thing the king thinks he can lavish on me now," Anne said with a sigh, waving her hand in the general direction of her desk.

"Come now, Anne, I saw the way he eyed you at court. He has eyes only for you. The queen hardly dines with him any longer and the whole court knows it. He desires a new mistress and anyone with eyes can see that he desires *you*," her father stated emphatically.

"I do not care a wit what he desires. I have made my intentions clear, and I will *not* be his mistress. I know of his desire. I witnessed his token at the joust on Shrove Tuesday. But I will not risk my reputation for his fleeting desires. Surely you must understand that, Father?" Anne asked.

"Anne, you must think of the family. Think of what favors he might bestow upon us. I know he has already graced you with trinkets. I heard tell of the golden whistle pendant he sent you from Mary. You will earn far more than just ornaments and jewels if he takes you to bed. We could earn lands; we could earn titles!" her father exclaimed.

"He does not love me. He loves what he cannot have. 'Tis all a game to him and he loves the chase," Anne said with a scowl deepening upon her pursed lips.

"Then play the game, Anne," her father said before flinging the gift upon the table and exiting.

Once her father had exited, she sat on her bed and let out a sigh. The package sat many feet away from her, yet still, she felt as though his seal were burning a brand into her skin, claiming her as his own. She felt like nothing more than a possession in his eyes. Yes, she had always wanted to be loved passionately and she had had that once with Henry Percy. But she was tired of men thinking no means yes. Even a king should be able to understand when his advances were not wanted!

She glanced at the gift a moment longer and it felt like it might sear a hole into her brain. *I will not open it. Will not! Let him know that his gifts are so far beneath me that I can't even bother to open them.*

With that thought she strode to her wardrobe and began examining the gowns she might wear for supper. She was at the task no more than a minute when curiosity got the better of her and she rushed to the desk, picked up the gift, and opened it with a flourish.

Inside the box sat a beautiful sapphire gem surrounded by gold filigree. The ring fit her finger beautifully and she knew it would look striking beside some of her best gowns. She sighed and removed the ring because as beautiful as the gift was, she did not want to accept it. She did not want to accept him. What did he not understand about that? She had run home to Hever to get away from his constant requests for her to be his mistress. Yet he continued trying to reach her as though she had never left.

She was starting to think if he was going to be so persistent about this, perhaps her father was right. Perhaps she *should* just succumb and use his love for her to her family's advantage. She may not love the man quite as ardently as he loved her, but that was no reason to stop herself from rising high.

A wicked gleam entered her eye as she wondered just how far she could rise with the king's love. She carefully slid the ring on her finger once more as she continued to ponder the king's affections.

May 1527

Anne climbed off of her horse and dusted off her skirts. She glanced upon Hever castle with a fondness she could only feel when she had been away for a while. She had always enjoyed court life but now that she was coyly dancing around Henry's advances there was an added intrigue that made it fun to stay. Spurning Henry's advances, while fun, had also been exhausting though so Anne was happy to have a reprieve here at her childhood home.

After being greeted by a bevy of servants and her family, she quickly excused herself to her room to change for dinner. Alone with her thoughts, she couldn't help but wonder if she'd made a mistake in agreeing to be Henry's official mistress. The light in his eyes when she'd agreed made her think, *maybe I could love this man.*

Of course, that light was soon followed by lust when she announced that she would not give herself to him until he could be hers completely before the eyes of God. She would not be his common whore and would only give herself to him once they could be married. She saw lust fill his eyes when she told him because he knew it meant that the chase was still on. The prize was not yet won but she was so close, and the temptation was driving him mad.

She wondered if it was right to lead him on so. Marriage was practically an impossibility and Katherine would never stand down. Would he finally tire of not being able to have her? Would he let her go? And did she even want that anymore?

True, she had never wanted to be seen as just an object, but the passion Henry showed her was beyond compare. And he could have any woman at court, but he chose to keep pursuing her. She had to admit, it made her feel captivating.

She did not like how muddled the king made her thoughts. She rested her head in her hands and sighed. What was she to do?

"Anne! A letter has arrived! And it's from the king!" her father announced excitedly as she entered the great hall.

"His infatuation for you grows," her father continued. "You made a smart move coming home when you did. Let him pine for you while you're away."

He handed the letter to her as he spoke, and she gripped it with trembling fingers. Fortunately, in his excitement, he didn't notice her trepidation.

She managed to paste on a calm yet austere mask as she said, "Father, please leave me. I must compose a response at once."

"As you wish, my dear," her father answered. A gleam lit his eye as if he could see his wealth unfolding with every word Anne penned.

Anne's hands continued to tremble as she dissected her emotions. A part of her felt elation. She was riding the high of being so desired. And he loved her so much and so powerfully that she could almost believe she loved him too. But a part of her still felt angry that sometimes it still felt like he only wanted to use her. And that anger fueled her to keep up this farce of asking for more and more. Yet another part of her was scared. What happened when the bubble of his love and desire for her popped? Would he cast her aside like he had her sister? Did she want that? Or would it break her heart? Frustration entered her mix of emotions as she struggled to find the answer.

Finally, she took a deep breath to compose herself, tore the letter open and read:

In turning over in my mind the contents of your last letters, I have put myself into great agony, not knowing how to interpret them, whether to my disadvantage, as you show in some places, or to my advantage, as I understand them in some others, beseeching you earnestly to let me know expressly your whole mind as to the love between us two.

It is absolutely necessary for me to obtain this answer, having been for above a whole year stricken with the dart of love, and not yet sure whether I shall fail of finding a place in your heart and affection, which last point has prevented me for some time past from calling you my mistress; because, if you only love me with an ordinary love, that name is not suitable for you, because it denotes a singular love, which is far from common. But if you please to do the office of a true loyal mistress and friend, and to give up yourself body and heart to me, who will be, and have been, your most loyal servant, (if your rigour does not forbid me) I promise you that not only the name shall be given you, but also that I will take you for my only mistress, casting off all others besides you out of my thoughts and affections, and serve you only. I beseech you to give an entire answer to this my rude letter, that I may know on what and how far I may depend. And if it does not please you to answer me in writing, appoint some place where I may have it by word of mouth, and I will go thither with all my heart. No more, for fear of tiring you. Written by the hand of him who would willingly remain yours,

H.R.

Her fingers lightly traced the words she'd just read, hovering over "with all my heart." It was clear that Henry wanted to give his all to her, but could she do the same? And he said he would cast every other woman aside so her path to the throne was becoming clearer and clearer each day. But when she got her crown, would all of this false love still be enough?

June 1527

My Mistress and Friend, my heart and I surrender ourselves into your hands, beseeching you to hold us commended to your favour, and that by absence your affection to us may not be lessened: for it were a great pity to increase our pain, of which absence produces enough and more than I could ever have thought could be felt, reminding us of a point in astronomy which is this: the longer the days are, the more distant is the sun, and nevertheless the hotter, so is it with our love, for by absence we are kept a distance from one another, and yet it retains its fervour, at least on my side; I hope the like on yours, assuring you that on my part the pain of absence is already too great for me; and when I think of the increase of that which I am forced to suffer, it would be almost intolerable, but for the firm hope I have of your unchangeable affection for me: and to remind you of this sometimes, and seeing that I cannot be personally present with you, I now send you the nearest thing I can to that, namely my picture set in a bracelet, with the whole of the device, which you already know, wishing myself in their place, if it should please you. This is from the hand of your loyal servant and friend,

H.R.

Tears sprang from her cheeks and for once she knew why. She felt complete adoration for this man who would give up so much so willingly just to be with her. He made her feel seen. He made her feel valued. She was beginning to think that it wouldn't be the worst thing if she went all in with him.

She clipped the bracelet on, smiling at the miniature likeness he'd sent. She reread his letter and began to feel the conviction rising within her.

July 1527

She had made her choice. If Henry would do anything to have her, even propose marriage, then so be it. She would accept his proposal.

She had furthered the chase by not allowing him to know her intimately until they shared a marriage bed and he had risen to the occasion. He had even gone so far as to seek an annulment from Katherine.

At the start, she had felt like nothing more than an object, a pretty prize for him to catch and tire of. But now that the catch was on the horizon and he still seemed so smitten, she was beginning to think maybe his devotion was true. Maybe it was her and only her in his eyes whether a chase commenced or not.

She felt so drawn to know him fully, to feel his devotion when he caressed her skin. She was so surprised to see the way her complex feelings kept shifting, but this proposal granted her high status and love, and she couldn't see anything wrong with that.

With her mind made up, she began to wrap the trinket she'd had designed for Henry a few weeks ago, when her resolve was beginning to fully form. She'd commissioned a jewel to be made of a golden ship housing a solitary damsel with a diamond on its bow.

The symbolism was so potent she could taste it. She was the damsel, jumping aboard Henry's boat, following the diamond that would lead to matrimony. The boat was so much more than a boat. It was a symbol of the rough seas ahead and her willingness to weather the storm with Henry through thick and thin.

She was all in, and Henry would know it when he received her gift. With that thought in mind, she smiled as she sent it off.

CHAPTER TWENTY-ONE

August 2019

He's here. The words repeated over and over again in Malorie's mind. She didn't have to ask any further questions. She could tell by the simultaneous shock, awe, and fear in her father's voice that he had locked eyes with King Henry VIII. And while she was happy that this piece of the puzzle was finally locking into place, she was frustrated that she went through the complicated process of getting into the Vatican library only for her journey to end in vain. It may just be teenage angst running through her, but she couldn't help but feel like it wasn't fair that she was forced to run all over Italy today, sweating in the heat and not speaking a lick of Italian, while her dad just got to take a thirty-minute car ride in a nice air-conditioned car, spend maybe five minutes checking in and getting to the object he needed, and voila, meet a ghost.

Well, better get a move on, she thought. To her father she said, "Great, I'll be on the next flight to London. Pick me up at the airport, will you?" She hung up abruptly after hearing his confirmation. She didn't want to linger any longer than necessary on the phone. She may be exhausted, but there was a whole new adventure to tackle, and she couldn't imagine ghosts would be willing to wait around while a sleepy teenager got a full night's rest.

London, England – Earlier that Day

Peter's knuckles were white against the steering wheel. He had to grip the leather as tightly as possible to keep his hands from shaking. He was mere minutes away from possibly seeing the ghost of the man he had studied for years. No amount of slow breathing could keep him calm in this moment.

He still marveled at the beautiful architecture in the London borough, as he pulled up to the white stone turrets that composed Strawberry Hill House. He had been here before and yet these structures never seemed to stop taking his breath away.

He couldn't believe he had probably looked at the clock he now sought dozens of times before but never had he asked to touch it. It was a well-known rule amongst historians that you never touched an artifact unless absolutely necessary lest you risk damaging it. He knew he would be granted access, as he was one of the leading historians on the Tudors, yet still he hesitated. Was he truly ready to face Henry if Henry's spirit really awaited him on the other side of those doors?

After showing his credentials and being led to the proper room he sat and waited. It felt like an eternity before an employee brought the clock to him, freeing it from its glass case.

He studied it intimately, still hesitant to touch it and still in awe of its sheer beauty. He had studied it behind the glass, he had studied pictures of it, yet still he marveled at the intricacies of the patterns atop it. He gazed lovingly at the 'H' and 'A' initials tied together with lovers' knots above the phrase 'The Most Happy.' He knew the most minute details of Henry and Anne's relationship and yet, to this day, he still puzzled over how someone could be so obsessively in love with someone and proceed to order their execution a few years later. He knew it was a matter of Henry's mental instability but as that was not an affliction he was burdened with, it was still hard for him to wrap his head around.

The thought of Henry's mental instability brought another reason for Peter's hesitation to his mind. What if Henry were still just as mad as he was when he died? Would Peter be putting himself in danger to bring him back? Could Henry even hurt him? Peter wasn't entirely sure of the mechanics behind being a ghost. And why would he be familiar? It's not like he'd encountered one before. While he was certain that there was no chance of Henry executing him as there were no execution scaffolds erected presently, he couldn't guarantee that Henry wouldn't somehow gain powers beyond incorporeality and find a way to push or strike him. Still, it was a risk he needed to take, and he knew it full-heartedly.

With that thought in mind, he touched the clock as lightly as possible so as not to leave a smudge. He instantly felt the cold breeze that accompanied Anne's appearance and stared wide-eyed at the figure of Henry VIII in front of him. He looked as he did in his prime, no obesity or ulcerated legs to ruin his figure.

Henry standing before him now made his jaw drop just as Malorie's had been doing all week. He struck an imposing figure with his broad shoulders and muscular arms. His ginger hair practically gleamed under his feathered cap. At this notice, Peter realized ghosts must come in color. Upon further reflection, he realized he had been able to see the rich, dark velvet of Anne's gown. Both ghosts appeared almost human but for a slight translucence to their presence.

Henry was adorned in jewels and clothes made of the most vibrant shades of red and gold. He wore an impressive, gilded codpiece that would have made any man or woman in today's world blush. His small lips were pursed, and his eyebrows scrunched as he glanced around at his surroundings, trying to place where he was. Peter was sure any minute now, Henry would realize Peter could see him by the way he was staring wide-eyed at him and attempt to initiate a conversation. Peter really needed to pull himself together.

Yet Peter was in such shock he could hardly pull his phone out of his pocket, let alone dial Mal's number. But he had to do this, he had to let her know they had found the missing piece of the puzzle. He simply croaked, "He's here" when he heard her pick up after the third ring. He couldn't manage to get any other words out. Was it normal for one's throat to close up when they met the man they had revered and studied for decades? Would he even be able to talk to the king he had spent half of his life studying? He sure hoped the shock of meeting the man he so admired wore off soon.

Malorie proceeded to mention flights back to London, but he was in such a daze he hardly registered her words. He hung up the phone and brought his attention back to the looming figure in front of him. He was getting the chance to talk to one of the most famed men in history and by God would he savor every second of it.

Who art thou? Henry asked. ***And where am I?***

Peter supposed now it was his turn once more to catch a centuries-old ghost up on present day matters. He had no clue how he hadn't lost his mind by now considering this was the third ghost he'd seen in as many days, but he supposed it would be best to try to keep his composure as he attempted a conversation with this famed king.

"Okay, um… bollocks," Peter started. He was afraid to even say a single word because he didn't want to come off as a nutter to a former king of England. That being said, the fact that he was seeing a former king of England standing in front of him might mean he was way too far gone to resemble anything close to sane anymore.

"Hi, I'm Peter," he tried again. His inclination was to reach out his hand for a shake, but he held back not only because it was not the custom in 16th century England, but because he knew his hand would feel like he had just stuck it in a bucket of ice water if he had.

"It's the year 2019 and you have been dead for nearly 500 years," he spoke slowly and gently. He couldn't imagine how disorienting it would be to reappear long after you had died in what essentially felt like a foreign world to you. The speech, dress, customs, and culture were so different from what Henry was used to and Peter feared his disorientation would lead to anger and that anger would lead to showcasing his mental instability.

What is this nonsense you speak of? Henry asked.

Okay, fair enough, Peter thought. *How do I prove to him that he's in the future?* In that moment, Peter had an epiphany as he whipped out his phone again. "See this device?" he asked as he slowly walked towards Henry, holding out his phone. "It has the time and date written right there on the screen."

Henry tried to reach for the phone, but his insubstantial hands merely passed right through it. ***What is this thing? Wherefore am I here?***

Good, good, Peter thought. *If he's asking why he's here it sounds like he's grasping the fact that he's out of his element. Maybe this will go smoother than I thought.*

"Okay, so, um, I think your spirit is attached to this clock," Peter said, holding up the clock in question. "The clock you gave to Anne Boleyn as a wedding present.".

Henry's face broke into equal parts rage and sadness over the name 'Anne Boleyn' and Peter had no trouble guessing why.

My Nan, my sweet, Henry said regret gleaming in his eyes. He looked like he wanted to reach towards the clock, to caress her initial A as his thoughts traveled back to their time together.

The way he spoke of Anne made it sound like he'd never married a third wife to replace her or three wives after that. Peter wondered what could possibly be going through his mind right now that he could be so enraptured with Anne and forget any of his other wives existed. He supposed love *could* blind you to everyone else in the world.

Wherefore am I here? Henry asked again, his voice laced with panic and confusion.

"Sometimes spirits become attached to this world because they have unfinished business, and they cannot pass on until the business is resolved. We, that is to say my daughter and I-she's who I was on the phone with earlier-we believe Anne is your unfinished business. My daughter came across Anne's spirit and we know *you* are *her* unfinished business. We think she is yours as well," Peter explained.

Henry looked at him as if he had two heads. This must be a confusing concept for a Protestant who didn't believe in purgatory. He must be wondering why his soul hadn't ascended to heaven. To think he had business with a wife he had long ago left behind after he anticipated going to heaven after his death and never ever seeing her again must be a very confusing prospect.

The mercy of God may pardon me all my sins, Henry answered as if in explanation for why he shouldn't be here, but Peter could hear the doubt in his voice and knew perhaps some sins and the guilt they carried were too grave for even death to cleanse.

Peter didn't know how to proceed from that sentence. "Well, that might be the case, but your spirit is here and so is Anne's, and it seems as though the both of you have some unresolved issues to address," Peter finally decided on a response. "My daughter is in possession of Anne's spirit. It's attached to the necklace with the B pendant that you gave her. She's on her way back to England. I suppose we'll have to bring the necklace here as I doubt, they'll let me take the clock with me, even with my credentials."

Peter knew he was babbling, and that Henry was probably barely processing any of his words, but he found babbling was the best way to make sense of everything and plan next steps.

He couldn't do anything else for Henry right now unless Henry was eager to chat with someone from a century so far removed from his own and Peter highly doubted that. Besides, the next part of the mission involved picking Malorie up from the airport; they couldn't finish this without bringing Henry and Anne together.

Before Henry could ask any more questions or preach about how he should be in heaven, not here, Peter said, "I have to go, but I'll be back. I promise." And with that, he returned the clock to its glass case and watched Henry dissolve in a swirl of mist.

CHAPTER TWENTY-TWO

⬦

If Malorie thought she was losing her sanity when she first saw Anne, she knew being in this airport would send any remaining dregs of sanity swiftly down the drain. She couldn't stand the crowds, the jostling, the chaos of it all. And, if she wasn't annoyed enough about having flown to Rome for no reason, the fact that she had to run all the way to the other side of the airport to find her gate surely would have done her in. Yes, she was aware that it was a very first world problem to be complaining about an impromptu trip to Italy, but it's not exactly like she could enjoy sightseeing with the stress of trying to get into one of the most coveted areas of the Vatican!

A week ago, Malorie never thought she'd be looking forward to seeing her dad again, because at that point she had spent a day with him and decided he was as dull as unbuttered toast, but now she was looking forward to being back in the UK and hearing all about his experience finding Henry's ghost.

Malorie boarded her flight and thought, *Finally God is blessing me,* as she realized she was granted a window seat and no passenger to sit beside her. Having to sit next to a snoring passenger or, God forbid, a crying baby for two hours would have sent Malorie over the edge. As it was, running through the airport and dealing with security had already driven her so crazy that she was currently dangling on the precipice of insanity.

Malorie glanced out the window to gaze at the sun and puffy clouds speckling the bright, blue sky of the Italian skyline and was amazed to find she was almost looking forward to the gray clouds and rain she was likely to experience as soon as the plane touched down in London.

Peter was waiting for her at baggage claim just as he promised, and Malorie couldn't help but smile. She had looked forward to seeing him and she hadn't expected her feelings to change so drastically towards him in just a week. She hadn't expected to feel like she might actually miss him as much as she'd been missing her mom and her friends throughout this whole vacation when she'd left.

After processing that thought, she realized she was a little surprised not to see the gold clock in Peter's hands and weirded out that she felt excited about touching the object and seeing Henry's ghost. *Get a grip, Malorie. Of course, he's not going to be carrying a centuries-old ornate clock around in an airport!* she chastised herself.

When they got into the car, she finally allowed herself to continue talking about solving the mystery of Henry and Anne; Anne's necklace was safely tucked inside her jacket pocket once again after her last trip through airport security, so they didn't need to worry about Anne listening in at the moment. "So, where is the clock? And what did Henry look like? How did he react? What did he say?" she rattled off question after question without pausing for breath.

She turned to her father and his eyes widened as if he had trouble processing her questions. She supposed she should slow down and let him catch his breath. She had so many questions following her first interaction with teaching a ghost about the twenty-first century that she was curious to see how her dad's experience had gone. But she was sure that lingering look of brain overload was likely the same look she had in her eyes when Anne first spoke to her. She almost forgot how practically traumatizing it was to meet a ghost for the first time, let alone a second time, and how you actually had to take a minute to let your brain catch up to the absurdity happening right before your eyes.

"He looked much as he did in his youth, big and strong and very intimidating, I might add," he started, chuckling to himself whether at his little joke or at the sheer insanity of this whole situation, it was hard to tell. Malorie supposed it could also be a nervous chuckle. Was there a sense of fear in Peter? And did that have to do with the fear of not living up to his idol's expectations? Or was it Henry himself who scared Peter? Malorie remembered that Henry was a very crazed man by the end of his life, and she wondered if that transferred to his ghost form.

"He looked as he did in his prime, much as Anne does to us. I think spirits must have a way of reflecting who the person was in their prime rather than who they were in death, otherwise Anne would have been headless to us this whole time," he finished. Malorie got wide-eyed at that picture and imagined how much extra therapy she'd need if the ghost that kept appearing to her was also headless. She couldn't help but imagine spectral blood spattering all over Peter's hardwood floors and she shuddered at the thought. Maybe she should lay off of horror movies for a while.

"And how did the whole 'hey, you've been dead almost 500 years and we need to bring you and Anne Boleyn face to face to solve this situation' talk go?" Malorie asked.

"Not nearly as hard as I anticipated. His biggest concern, once he got over having his spirit brought to the future, was his internal conflict over his soul still being here. He seemed genuinely convinced that he should be in heaven by now. Which I suppose is a sensible reaction from someone who used religion to justify his original annulment and who made himself Supreme Head of the Church of England," Peter mused.

Malorie glanced in the back seat of the car, expecting to find the clock in Peter's possession still. Sure, a part of her thought fancy, ancient relics probably couldn't leave the museums they were housed in, but she also thought Peter might be such a fancy-pants historian that he could take out whatever relic he wanted from whatever museum he wanted.

"Soooo… why is it you don't have the clock on you anymore?" she asked.

"I might have many credentials that give me a lot of access to historical objects, but I can only pull so many strings. The clock can't leave Strawberry Hill House which means we'll have to go back. But we've been through enough for the past day and a half so I was thinking we could start the next stage of the mission tomorrow. What do you say to that, love?" Peter asked.

"I think, after running like a mad woman through an Italian airport, I am definitely ready to call it a day here and start fresh tomorrow," Malorie answered with a sigh.

Chapter Twenty-Three

The Wednesday afternoon sun shone bright through Malorie's bedroom window, and Malorie awoke to drool gracing her face and bedhead that would put a bird's nest to shame. Not a pretty sight. The smell of coffee wafted from the kitchen, which told her Peter had been up since dawn if he was sipping on the strongly caffeinated beverage. He only ever drank it when he was extremely tired. She wondered if thoughts of the impending reconciliation between Anne and Henry had kept him up all night. She knew it would have for her if she weren't so utterly confident that *this* was exactly what they needed to solve the problem that lingered between the spirits. She may not have gone through very many relationships of her own, being only sixteen and all, but she was pretty sure people everywhere, from the poorest of folks to kings and queens, had an easier time moving on from relationships when some form of closure was found. She also thought no amount of anxious thoughts keeping her brain from turning off could have possibly kept her awake last night. Her body was so physically tired from running all over Rome that by the time her head hit the pillow, her eyelids felt like anchors weighing her down and she'd have had to have had super-strength to keep them wide open.

Malorie was almost afraid to have the spirits come face to face, not because she feared any danger between the two of them, but because she knew once this was solved, she'd have to head back to America. She wasn't even sure how much she wanted to head back to America now, not only because of her growing love for her dad but because she was in no hurry to have the possibly relationship-ending conversation that she needed to have with Robbie. But she had to admit, she probably should fear *some* amount of danger between the two of them considering one had the other beheaded. You didn't just get over that even if almost 500 years had passed!

She walked into the kitchen, bed hair still intact and pajamas still rumpled to ask her dad, "So what's the game plan for today? Do we just go straight back to the clock with the necklace and hope talking can get them both where they need to be? Do we bring anything as a safety precaution in case things go awry? 'Cuz I've watched enough *Supernatural* to know that a gun loaded with salt pellets should do the trick! And if we smell sulfur, we better run!"

Peter looked at her as though she had gone insane at the mention of *Supernatural* and said, "I think we need to bring Anne out this morning to prepare her for seeing him again and help her figure out what to say to him."

"Yeah, it'll be just like when you coax your bestie through a breakup, no biggie," Malorie commented wryly.

"Now's not the time for jokes, love," Peter said, taking up the sternest dad voice he had given her all week. "Let's enjoy our breakfast and then we can bring Anne out in a bit."

It went just as expected and Malorie was not sure how she *still* hadn't gotten accustomed to that blast of cold air yet. She was looking down at the goose pimples on her arm when she heard Anne ask, **Where is he? I wish to speak to him!**

Malorie supposed she shouldn't be surprised that the next time she and her father brought Anne's essence around that Anne's first query would be about Henry. After all, they told her they'd try to help her spirit pass by letting her and Henry have a heart-to-heart, and that conversation couldn't really take place without the mad king in question.

Peter decided to answer her on this one. "We've found his location. He's attached to the golden clock he gave you as a wedding present. Unfortunately, we couldn't take the clock home with us, which means we need to take you to the clock," Peter answered.

Well, why am I not at this location now? Let us make haste, Anne growled. Malorie was wondering if she sounded more cross merely because her anger was shining through at the thought of facing Henry again so soon.

"We can't remove his object from its location. We must bring you to Strawberry Hill House to see him. It's about a thirty-minute ride," Peter explained.

Well, we must leave at once then, Anne answered. Malorie didn't think there was any sense arguing with her on the topic, so she merely grabbed her bag, stuffed the necklace inside as well as a bottle of water and a granola bar in case she got snacky.

She looked up at Peter to see a confused expression on his face. She looked around to see dirty dishes in the sink and half-filled coffee mugs on the table. She had almost forgotten they had been in the middle of breakfast. Anne had such a commanding voice that Malorie heard her words and instinctively reacted to obey.

"Oh, sorry Peter. I suppose we should clean up first," Malorie mumbled apologetically.

Peter replied, "No, I suppose she's right after all. The sooner we solve all of this, the better everyone will feel. We better get going if we want to solve this for good."

Pulling up to Strawberry Hill House a half hour later, Malorie's eyes widened in surprise. How was it that nearly every structure in England could somehow look like Hogwarts? The bright, white façade and the tall steeples made her feel like she was about to enter yet another castle.

She wasn't sure how ready she was to meet King Henry VIII. Granted, she didn't know much about him but from what her dad told her, he was a tall and imposing figure with a bad temper, and she was not eager to try to have a conversation with that. Especially as she knew Anne's temper could be just as bad. She'd rather stay out of the middle of it all.

Malorie and her father were escorted to the case that held the clock without issue and Malorie was, once again, glad that her father was a celebrated historian with highly sought-after credentials who could get them through places like this with minimal hurdles.

The clock was a marvelous sight to behold, and Malorie had to will her jaw not to drop yet again. *Jeez, my jaw will be sore by the time I leave England if I keep this up,* she thought, and chortled to herself.

The clock was ornate and delicate in a way that objects today could never fully master. Just looking at it felt like looking at something ancient and magical, like King Arthur's sword ready to be pulled from the stone. It looked like the creator had spent hours, days, or possibly even *years* slaving over this creation, pouring his whole heart and soul into each golden curve. Malorie had to remind herself not to let her fingers lightly trace the entwined H and A carved into the clock because she wasn't ready for Henry's company just yet.

"How are we gonna do this?" she asked, turning back to her dad.

"Well, I've already asked for and guaranteed us full privacy so we won't look like complete nutters talking to ghosts that nobody else can see," her dad responded.

"Well, that's a step in the right direction at least," Malorie acknowledged. "So, I think we're both going to have to be touching both objects at the same time in order to see both ghosts and act as mediators of a sort." She almost surprised herself with the level of authority in her voice. What did she know about being a ghost counselor? Enough to facilitate and direct this conversation, apparently.

"I think that's a great idea," Peter replied.

Peter carefully brought the clock out of its glass case and set it on the table before them, careful to use a cloth for preservation purposes as well as to ensure Henry's ghost didn't come calling before they were ready for him. Malorie set the necklace on the table, careful to keep the handkerchief wrapped around it so as not to call Anne before they were ready to speak to her.

"You ready to do this?" Peter asked, a gleam of excitement and nervous anticipation in his eye.

Malorie could feel the knot in her stomach growing as she answered, "Not really, but what choice do we have?" With that, Malorie removed the handkerchief and pressed the necklace against the clock, making sure she had a firm hand on both just as her father did. Henry and Anne appeared simultaneously in a swirl of cold mist, locked eyes, and attempted to launch at each other.

Chapter Twenty-Four

It was clear from the way they moved towards each other that they did not have the same thoughts running through their minds. Henry looked as if he were launching himself at Anne in order to pick her up and hug her to him tightly, as if it was just now dawning on him how much he missed her after all of these years apart. Meanwhile, Anne launched herself at Henry as though she were a predator ready to attack her prey. The fierce, deranged gleam in her eye made it clear that she was out for blood and would claw her way through him if she must. Henry, being so madly in love with her, as he had been from the start, must not have recognized the delirious look on her face for what it was, pure intent to murder.

It was all for naught though. As the two bodies attempting to collide were incorporeal, they simply passed through each other in a cloud of mist. This did nothing to abate Anne's anger.

How dare you show your face after what you have done! Thank God mine own spirit was restored to mine own body otherwise you would be staring at a corpse holding her head in her hands, Anne declared, and it looked like it was taking all of her energy not to launch herself at Henry again. *You'd have me reduced to a gruesome horror with naught but a twinkle in your eye just so that Seymour whore could take my place! What of the love you once bore me? Where was that as I sat upon the execution block?* Anne pleaded, hints of rage and despair coloring her words. Malorie was surprised she didn't see flecks of phantom spittle flying as Anne fumed.

Malorie had been expecting her or Peter to have to start the conversation to get the two talking, but it was clear that Anne was ready to face her greatest love and torment once and for all.

Nan, it was nothing more than a plot to see the monarchy survive. You have no conceit what it cost me to have you removed. 'Tis why I could not bear to see you one last time. I knew I would change mine own mind and I could not allow mine own love for you to thwart the chances of the monarchy, Henry answered in a booming voice, his eyes promising all of the sincerity his words claimed. Peter noticed he started with his nickname for her and couldn't help but thinking it was a bold choice considering she still looked ready to tear his head off.

They told me about your fourth wife! she screamed, pointing at Peter and Malorie with her declaration. *The one you divorced and made thy 'sister.' Why couldn't that have been mine own fate?* Anne asked. Her voice trembled and Malorie sensed it was for all that could have been if she had been allowed to live.

Dear, we both know you ne'er would have relented so calmly and quietly, Henry answered, showing a calm he had not shown previously, likely in an effort to keep Anne calm as well.

Maybe so. But I wouldst have lik'd to have been given the option, Anne responded, her former regal demeanor returning to her presence.

And what of my dear, sweet cousin, Katherine Howard? Anne continued. *They told me you took her as your fifth wife, and she met the same deadly end as me. A young and naïve child, she was. Surely, she would have calmly stepped down as your fourth wife did?* Anne challenged him. Malorie could tell that Anne's questioning of her cousin's fate meant she wanted answers from Henry not just about her own cruel end, but about all of the atrocities he committed as he transformed into the monster he was in his later years. Perhaps Anne, too, wanted the score settled not just for herself, but for every scorned lover out there.

Is it merely Howard blood you wished to shed? Anne continued. *Were you still so repulsed by the memory of me that you had to execute where you still saw the resemblance?* she asked.

Henry shook, whether from rage or sadness it was hard to tell, that is until he opened his mouth. *How dare you question the motives of a king?! I only ever did what I needed to for kingdom and country! She committed treason. I could not let her live. She was young and had no head for ruling. I was blinded by her beauty. But she fooled me greatly. And I never loved her like you. There was proof beyond measure for her crimes against me and the crown. Far more than was ever mustered for you. I could not let her live.* He sounded sad, likely sad for the way events played out and sad for the loves he lost.

So, you ne'er believed the rumors about the affairs, did you? Because I ne'er once strayed from you. Malorie could hear in Anne's voice how badly she wanted him to believe her, perhaps because he was so resolutely against her before.

I know, mine own love. And I am sorry. I had to maintain a pretense in order to—

Help the monarchy survive, Anne finished. *I know. But I could have bore you a son,* Anne declared defiantly. But her eyes shone bright with unshed tears and everyone in the room could tell she was thinking what she spoke out loud just a few days ago, that she thought herself broken and it killed her that she had failed where plain Jane Seymour had succeeded.

Mine own sweet Nan, we both know it was too late. After all of the miscarriages and stillbirths, God had fated us not meant to be, Henry answered solemnly. It broke his heart that Anne never gave him the son he needed. He never wanted to get rid of her. But he couldn't deny that success followed in her wake so it must have been the right choice.

Peter found it necessary to chime in here, adding, "Actually, Henry, historians and scientists today have been able to almost definitively confirm that you had Kell positive blood, and all of your wives had Kell negative blood. Without getting into too much scientific detail that would likely go beyond you, your attempt to conceive with women who did not share the Kell positive blood type made it easy for you to conceive initially but much more difficult for any proceeding offspring to survive."

Henry looked like he was ready to rip Peter's head off as he said, *But I beget a son. God granted me a son. How dare you accuse me of being debased? I am a king, remember!*

Malorie could see that Henry's old temper was back as he shouted this. He likely wanted to rip Peter's head off for speaking ill against a king. Men were killed for less where Henry came from.

Peter continued, "I am sorry, King Henry. I meant no offense. And yes, you did have a son with Jane Seymour. It is mostly considered pure luck that that was able to happen."

Malorie could see the way Henry practically deflated at her father's words and she almost felt bad for the guy. Almost being the key word there; no way was she letting him off the hook for beheading and divorcing so many wives. Malorie looked at Anne and it almost appeared that Anne had a gloating gleam in her eye. Malorie supposed she too would feel the need to gloat if after all of these years of being told she was lesser than and practically a witch for marrying a king and failing to have a son, she finally found out it was the *king* who was broken. And maybe she was too but at least Henry could not escape the blame so easily.

Anne spoke up at that moment to say, ***Wha! So, you have fail'd as much as me, the plain, little Seymour whore aside.*** She was practically manic in her conviction, but boy did she glow in her self-righteousness. ***Seymour girl or no, I did not deserve to be set aside and you know that.***

But she beget me a son. She allow'd the monarchy to thrive in a way you didst not, Anne. I am sorry. But it had to be. God will'd it, Henry answered.

Well God will'd mine own daughter to rule for forty-five years. A glorious rule she had. Tell him, Anne demanded, pointing to Peter once again. Of course, it was just like Anne to make sure she had a counterpoint to every comment that Henry threw her way.

"She is correct, King Henry. Elizabeth ruled for 45 years and had one of the most successful reigns of the English kingdom. She oversaw many expeditions, defeated the Spanish Armada, and allowed Protestantism to rule the land, among other things," Peter answered.

Peter and Malorie saw the gleam of pride in Henry's eye before he asked, ***And what of mine own Edward? Was his rule just as prosperous?***

Peter hated to disappoint the king, but he had to answer honestly. "I'm sorry, Your Majesty. He died just six years after your own death at the age of fifteen. It is widely believed that he died from tuberculosis."

An opaque tear slid down Henry's jowly cheek. He whispered, ***Mine own brother, Arthur, died at fifteen too. Curse fate for repeating itself.***

Henry continued, ***Well, Arthur was married at fifteen and likely consummated the marriage. Didst Edward at least marry? Didst he*** *beget any children? Dost the Tudor name live on?* He asked in quick succession. Henry seemed to be fearful of hearing the answer but the twinkle in his eye showed he was eager for the truth.

"I'm sorry, Your Majesty. Edward did not have any children. Nor did Mary or Elizabeth. The Tudor name ended with Elizabeth's reign and from there passed to James Stuart, crowned James VI of Scotland, and James I of England. He was your sister Margaret's great-grandson," Peter explained to Henry.

In that moment they all saw the absolute heartbreak cross Henry's face. Malorie figured it was likely because everything he had worked so hard to achieve hadn't even lasted. And maybe he realized it hadn't even mattered that he had finally had the son he so longed for when his daughter had ended up having a longer and better rule than Edward anyhow! Maybe he could finally see how he was at fault and how neither Anne nor Katherine deserved to be discarded the way they were. She imagined that he could only imagine what his future might have been like if he had accepted Elizabeth for the queen she would one day be and let Anne, his beloved Anne, remain his queen until the end of his days. Maybe he wouldn't be a spirit currently locked out of heaven if he could have avoided all of the sins that had placed him here.

Henry strode towards Anne and let his ghostly hands rest just above her shoulders, the closest he could possibly come to touching her. He then said, *I am sorry, mine own sweet Nan. I am so, so sorry. You were right and always have been. I have ne'er loved anyone as I have loved you. I wish I had known what I was sacrificing. Mine own heir was ne'er more important than you and I am glad Elizabeth had such a long and productive reign*.

For the first time since Malorie had met her, she saw Anne smile. It was a genuine wide-mouthed beam that lit up her face. Malorie knew that at last Anne was hearing the words she needed to hear all those centuries ago. Henry was beaming just as widely, an exuberant laugh escaping his lips as he got to see her smile. Malorie stared at the couple. She saw a glimmer of peace in Anne's eyes and a glimmer of love in Henry's. They held each other as best they could for a few more seconds before they both slowly dissolved from toes to head. Malorie couldn't help but be reminded of the Thanos snap from *The Avengers* as she watched them dissolve because that's what this was like, not like the swirl of mist she was used to seeing. Their transparent bodies chipped away, looking like ash floating on the nonexistent breeze. The last thing she saw was the look of absolute joy and awe in both of their eyes before they disappeared entirely.

Malorie glanced down to see that she and Peter were still holding the artifacts, yet she felt no tingle up her fingers or cold breeze pushing her hair off her face. She knew without having to feel it that Henry and Anne had finally passed on and the issue was resolved. No longer would she have a 16th century queen yelling at her. She could finally return home to a *normal* life with *normal* friends and her *normal* mom.

"Well," she said as she looked up to lock eyes with Peter, "I think our work here is done."

"Too right you are," he replied. And with that they placed the clock back in its glass case and left Strawberry Hill House.

CHAPTER TWENTY-FIVE

Malorie could still sense the bulge of the necklace in her pocket and yet she felt this indescribable lightness surrounding it, almost as if the weight of the world was no longer on her shoulders. The heaviness of Anne's heart was no longer weighing her down.

"So, what are we gonna do with this thing?" she turned to her dad to ask as she ran the pearls through her fingers, marveling at the fact that she could do this now without raising goosebumps all along her skin. The British countryside rolled past, and she glimpsed sun and blue skies. She knew it might be wishful thinking, but a part of her hoped the clouds had parted because Henry and Anne had finally made it into heaven.

Her father pulled her out of that thought by answering, "I think the best thing we could do is donate that to a museum anonymously, and I think I know just the place to do it."

Malorie and her father sat around his kitchen table sipping tea. It was a mirror image of the way her week had started when he picked her up at Heathrow all of those days ago. For a second, Malorie had to pinch herself to make sure she hadn't dreamed the whole ghostly excursion.

Her hand instinctively went to her jacket pocket, and she felt a sense of emptiness, like a hole in her heart, over feeling no lump in her pocket. All that remained was lint.

Her father had decided the best place to send the necklace would be to the Chequers estate so the necklace could join Elizabeth I's ring that contained a portrait of Elizabeth and a portrait of her mother, Anne Boleyn. Peter felt sure that's where Anne would have wanted her belongings to rest. If the necklace could not rest upon her daughter's shoulders, then he could give her the next best thing and have it rest beside her daughter's possessions.

Peter had stated as much in the letter he wrote to be delivered with the package that contained the necklace. He made sure to write it in a handwriting that could not be matched to his own and wore gloves as he wrote so no fingerprints could be traced back to him. As much as he wanted to lay claim to having Anne Boleyn's precious necklace in his possession, he just didn't think he could handle the barrage of questions that would ensue. Considering the necklace had been lost since Anne's death nearly 500 years ago, there was no plausible explanation he could come up with that justified, "Uh, I just stumbled across it." He was afraid he might be taken to court or even to prison if the authorities thought he had been hiding stolen treasures on his person this whole time. No, better to deliver it anonymously and get it out of his hair.

As much as he wanted to hold onto the necklace himself, put it on display, or caress those soft, aging pearls every chance he got, he knew he owed it to budding historians and Tudor fans everywhere to let them have a peek at this resurfaced necklace.

He was glad the necklace would be safe next to Elizabeth's possessions, on display in a museum with no ghost attached to it and no chance of any innocent victims getting hurt. What he was not glad for was that now that the mystery was solved, Malorie was set to fly back to America the next day.

He loved her from the moment he held her as a babe to the moment he set eyes on her exiting the airport terminal when she first arrived to this moment right now, where he could gaze upon the serene expression on her face and know she was at peace now that the necklace conundrum was solved. He'd never stopped loving her and he never would. He knew why she had been cold and distant to him at the start, and he couldn't really blame her. He never should have left his family behind, and he'd spend the rest of his days trying to make it up to her if he could.

He felt like this ghostly expedition had drawn them closer and he hoped she felt it too. He noticed how she had started calling him 'dad' sometimes and he hoped that wasn't just some common courtesy on her end but rather a name she genuinely wanted to call him.

"I hope you had—,"

"I think I want—," they both started at the same time.

"Sorry, you go first, love," Peter said.

"I think I want... that is... I wouldn't mind coming to visit you again sometime... if you'd be okay with that?" Malorie stumbled over her words, the last part coming out as a question.

Peter could hardly hold back his tears. This is what he'd been dreaming of hearing from the moment he saw her again, teenage Malorie this time around instead of toddler Malorie. All he'd wanted was to get her to understand what drew him to London over a decade ago. He'd been pulled here like London was the world's strongest magnet and he'd been determined to show her why he never could resist the pull. It's why he showed her all of the history he could possibly manage in a week's time. He never thought Anne Boleyn's ghost would be the reason she stayed but he was beyond grateful for going through that spiritual ordeal if it meant she'd want to come back and see him again sometime.

"Sure, Mal, I'd love that," he said, hoping she didn't hear the way his voice almost broke over the words. Dads were not cool if they showed way too much emotion over loving their daughters, after all.

She didn't flinch when he slipped up and used his nickname for her and he hoped it was because she was finally comfortable with it and with him. He was afraid to admit it, but the way she smiled at him contentedly made him think maybe she had finally let go of all of her anger towards him. Maybe she had finally found space in her heart to love him the way he loved her.

"I'll call your mum when you get back and we can work out arranging a trip sometime later in the year. And I'll have to make sure it doesn't conflict with any conferences or travel I have to do for work. But I'd love to have you back, more than anything," he said, and he couldn't stop his voice from wavering this time.

"Ah, dad, don't get all mushy on me," Malorie joked as she sat up and gave Peter the hug he'd been looking forward to receiving the whole week she'd been with him.

"You best go pack, love. You have an early flight tomorrow and I want you to be prepared and well-rested"

"I know, dad, I know," she spoke softly, with more tenderness and affection in her voice than he'd ever had the privilege of hearing. She smiled at him, and he finally saw the love in her eyes he'd been craving to see all along. She continued, "Thank you, dad. And... I love you. I can't believe I'm saying this, but I'm really grateful I came on this trip." She placed a kiss on his cheek and, with that, walked out the door and towards her room, leaving behind the scent of her vanilla shampoo.

Chapter Twenty-Six

The jolt of wheels hitting the tarmac roused Malorie from her sleep. The sleep lines on her face and drool adorning her pillow told her she had been in a deep sleep, and she silently cursed herself knowing how jet lagged she'd feel later.

Aside from the sleep, she felt mildly melancholic. All week, she had been looking forward to seeing JFK again and knowing she was just a short ride away from being home for good. But now that the airport loomed in front of her, she couldn't help wishing she had never said goodbye to Heathrow.

The tears staining her father's cheeks as he gave her one last hug were enough to make her start crying as well. She hated showing emotion of any kind, but she just couldn't help it. She had grown to love the man who was meant to be in her life this whole time. And as angry as she had been that he had abandoned her and her mom for so long, a part of her was grateful he was making up for lost time now. The fact that she had her opportunity to vent and scream at him combined with the fact that he had gotten the opportunity to express to her that the separation wasn't entirely one-sided, had been just what the two of them needed to heal. And the two weeks she had spent with him had really shown her just how much she meant to him. She was finally able to put some perspective on the situation and realize she had pushed him away so he wouldn't have the chance to do the same to her. In realizing this, she had also realized that he had never *wanted* to push her away; she had let her fears speak for themselves all these years.

With their last hug goodbye, she promised to visit again soon. And she knew this time she wasn't speaking from a place of idle pleasantries, she truly meant it. He'd choked out a last goodbye in between sobs and suggested she visit him on her next school break. She promised to take him up on that offer, although next time she hoped there would be less ghostly interference.

Her mother waited for her in baggage claim as promised and Malorie ran to embrace her in the biggest bear hug the world had ever seen. Her mother laughed as she stroked her hair and jokingly commented, "Looks like someone is happy to see me."

"Mom, you have no idea how much I've missed you!" Malorie exclaimed.

"Then why did you want more time with your dad? That's the part I can't quite wrap my head around. You didn't seem too eager to see him at the start of this trip. I'm sorry I pushed you…" Her mom trailed off, seeing that Malorie was in the middle of pulling her suitcase from the carousel and was clearly distracted.

"No, mom. The trip was great. I had loads of fun. Dad's really not so bad," Malorie said, trying to lighten the mood with a humorous tone. She continued, "And to answer your question, I just really got into British history while I was there and needed a longer vacation to soak it all in."

Malorie's mom looked at her with a quizzical expression but didn't ask any further questions. Malorie knew she was likely thinking about every F Malorie had brought home from history class as the puzzled look spread across her face and although she opened her mouth as if to protest, she ultimately remained silent for which Malorie was extremely grateful.

"Soooo, are you excited to hang with Robbie again?" her mom asked.

"C'mon, mom, nobody says hang anymore! You really need to get with the times," Malorie said with a chuckle. "But yeah, I told Robbie that I'd meet him at the mall tomorrow. Would you mind dropping me off?"

Her mother gave her a stern look. She hated when Malorie made plans last minute, but she supposed she had to give her a break. It *was* still summer break after all. And the only reason Malorie didn't drive herself is because she was adamant that Malorie hold off on getting her license. She knew the crowd Malorie hung around with could be a little reckless, and she didn't want her girl getting caught in a foolish accident due to peer pressure and/or plain old poor teenage decision-making skills.

"Okay, but you know curfew is 10:00pm and you better not break it," she warned.

"Yes, mom! Got it," Malorie said with as much teenage angst as a teenager could put into a sentence.

"For now, let's just get you home and have you get some sleep. That jet lag's going to catch up with you pretty soon. And I'll even help you unpack," her mom said, wrapping an arm around Malorie's shoulders as she guided her to the car.

Malorie couldn't deny, she'd spent a lot of time daydreaming about her Tempur-Pedic mattress and her plush pillows, especially after briefly experiencing the travesty that Anne's 16th century bed had been. She thought about how much she couldn't wait to lie in her bed again the whole trip home.

She uttered a curt hello to her stepdad, Marc. As she entered the house and scrambled upstairs to her bedroom. As tired as she was, she couldn't let the airplane grime she felt permeating her whole body infect her bed, so she rushed herself to the shower. After a deep cleanse of her body and deep condition of her hair, she was ready to wrap herself in her gloriously soft blankets.

She lay there, taking note that no scary wind was blowing her hair from her face and no ghost was whispering eerie ancient words in her ear in a vengeance-fueled tone.

These past few days with Anne had been one heck of a roller coaster ride. As scared and frustrated as the whole experience had made her, she wouldn't trade it for the world. It had been harrowing, sure, but Malorie and her father had completed the most badass quest in the world, reconciling an ancient queen's murder, and had come out on the other side stronger for it. Most importantly, Anne finally knew peace now. Malorie must find her peace too and unfortunately, she knew the only way she'd find it was by finally having the conversation she needed to have with Robbie tomorrow. As peaceful as she felt about Anne, she couldn't deny there was a pit of dread in the middle of her stomach at the thought of what awaited her tomorrow.

Malorie slurped her Diet Coke with a lot more calm than she felt inwardly. "Thanks for meeting me here," Malorie said, gesturing to the Sbarro that stood mere feet from the table she and Robbie currently occupied. She thought her voice sounded a lot more cheery than she truly felt.

"No prob," Robbie muttered. She noticed that he didn't even call her babe or any other term of endearment. The least he could have done was say her name!

He dug into the fries he had gotten from the Burger King on the other side of the food court with gusto. He never once made eye contact as he vigorously dipped his fries in Ranch.

Malorie sighed heavily. She hoped maybe it was a fluke and she had imagined his lack of attention this whole time. She hoped maybe just because she was hundreds of miles away and missing him even more than usual that physical distance could account for emotional distance. But here she was now, close enough to lay her hand on his, and she still missed him the same. He had changed so much since he had started his college program.

Malorie sighed once more. There was nothing for it but to rip the Band-Aid off. Yet she was terrified of the pain that would ensue. She could only sigh so many times and still not get his attention, so she finally said, "Robbie, I think we need to talk."

"We are talking, babe," he said casually, licking his fingers of fry grease.

"No, Robbie, I mean actually talk. I need more than five words from you for this conversation," she said a little sternly and a lot more seriously.

Robbie, appearing to finally detect the tone in her voice, looked up, wide-eyed.

"What's wrong?" he asked.

"You tell me," she answered. "Ever since you went to that college program you've barely paid any attention to me. I get that you're busy, but you could at least take ten minutes out of your day to devote yourself to a conversation with me! You haven't done that in *months!*"

"I'm sorry, babe. What do you want from me? I have classes all day and then homework that takes all night to do," Robbie answered sheepishly.

"Then why is it that sometimes when I call, I can hear your guy friends laughing it up in the background, asking you to play beer pong and what not. Is that part of your studying, Robbie?" Malorie asked, anger coloring her words. It was one thing for Robbie to make excuses, it was another thing for him to lie all together. Malorie knew she was glaring and hoped that Robbie was internally cowering with fear, thinking, "if looks could kill, I'd be a goner for sure!"

"Come on, babe. I've been working so hard. I can't have fun every once in a while?" he asked innocently.

"It sounds like it's more than once in a while to me," Malorie answered. "And since it sounds like you have more free time than you had previously alluded to, I still can't understand why you can't use some of that free time towards me. You used to bring me flowers and write me notes. You made a point to always have a date night every Friday. And I get it if you can't devote quite as much time to me, but I still feel there should be some compromise. Maybe I don't see you every Friday, but why not once or twice a month instead?"

"Uhhhh, I don't know, babe," Robbie answered, shrugging his shoulders.

Malorie waited for him to continue. She thought her solution was the perfect compromise and couldn't fathom why it would not work. After a few minutes of watching him nervously comb through his hair and look anywhere but at her, she asked, "What don't you know, Robbie?"

"Uhhhhh," he answered once more.

"Why wouldn't it work? I'm asking for two days a month of your attention and you can't even give me that?" Malorie asked. Her voice was beginning to crack, and she could feel her throat tightening as the tears threatened to pour. But she was determined to not break down in this food court. Sob if she must on the car ride home, sure, but she would not allow Robbie to make her look a fool in public.

"Uhhhh, I mean I'm busy. Like, I-"

"You are not so busy that you can't see me twice a month. You can take a break from beer pong and see me for a night. You could if you wanted to. You just don't. And why don't you, Robbie? I still can't quite wrap my head around it," Malorie interjected.

"I don't know, babe. You're just… you're not at college so you couldn't get it. It's like a whole different world out there, babe. I don't have time for silly high school stuff anymore."

"So, I am silly high school stuff to you, huh? What happened to wanting to date long distance while I stayed in high school and you went to college? We talked about the degrees we wanted. How we'd pursue them and, when we had enough money from our careers, we'd buy a house and a dog. That's all silly high school stuff now, Robbie?" Malorie asked.

"Come on, babe. Don't be like that. We both know that's not realistic. But once you're in college, you'll get it, you'll see. You'll just want to be free," Robbie answered, a wistful gleam in his eye as if he was imagining being back on campus this very minute.

"You want to be free of me, Robbie?" Malorie asked. She was clenching her jaw so hard she thought it might crack.

"Babe, that's not what I said," Robbie said exasperatedly.

"You didn't have to say it, Robbie. I can read between the lines loud and clear. And don't call me babe anymore. I'm more than happy to set you *free* if that's what you want!" Malorie said, her voice rising to just below shouting levels.

She threw her napkin on the table as she stood up and walked out.

Malorie sat on the curb, tears streaming down her face as she waited for her mom to pick her up. Robbie hadn't followed her out of the food court, hadn't chased her down through the mall, hadn't even called or sent a text in the thirty minutes since she had stormed off. She knew it was really over. And while a part of her mourned for the Robbie who sent her flowers in high school, another part knew he'd never be that guy again. He was in a college state of mind now, a freer state as he had put it. And somehow, as devastated as she was, she felt freer too. She felt free to not be tied down by men who didn't care about her anymore, just like Anne had. And although Anne's was a happier confrontation, Malorie felt a twinge of pride in her chest that she could now say she had faced the man who had hurt her head on, just like Anne. They had both learned peace from the confrontation too. Malorie smiled at the thought and wiped her tears away.

EPILOGUE

September 2019

Malorie stared at the somewhat lumpy package clutched tightly between her fingers. She had been in a bit of a daze since retrieving the mail. She had absentmindedly wandered into her bedroom and sat at the edge of her bed, holding the package aloft. That was an hour ago. Yet here she still sat, arms extended, staring wide-eyed at the large, looping g's and super curvy a's on the parcel in front of her.

She had received a few letters from Peter since she had gotten home so she knew this was from him, that's not what concerned her. She had been in a daze since touching the package because this wasn't like Peter's normal letters. This package was lumpy and felt oddly like a pearl necklace.

Dread raced through her in the form of a chill snaking its way through her veins. *Why did he send me this?* she thought. *Anne is gone so why the heck would he bring her back?*

It took all of her might to tear the package open and let the contents spill into her open palm. It was, just as she suspected, a pearl necklace with a gold B attached. But she knew something was off the moment it touched her skin. For one, there was no blast of cold air and for two, these didn't feel quite like the pearls she'd remembered holding for a week straight. Were these even real?

She took a close look and noticed that the pearls appeared to be made of plastic or some similar material. The golden B wasn't so cheaply made, but it was definitely not real gold, merely some knock-off material.

It's not real! she exclaimed internally. *It's just a replica.* She couldn't help sighing with relief at the realization. That's when she noticed that a slip of

161

paper had fallen to the floor as she'd deposited the necklace into her hand. With shaking fingers, (she was still riding the adrenaline high from the big necklace reveal) she unfolded the piece of paper and read:

Dear Mal,

Hope I didn't give you too much of a fright by sending you this necklace. I realize you may have feared I was sending Anne back to you but have no worries. The __real__ necklace is still safely secured in Chequers estate and though I have visited the necklace many times myself, Anne has not reappeared to me. I think she has safely passed on with Henry, just like we intended for her.

I took a visit to Hever Castle, Anne's birthplace, and home estate, and stumbled upon a store selling replicas of Anne's beloved necklace. I couldn't help but buy one for you. After all we went through with the necklace in question, I thought you might like to have one for yourself, one that doesn't have a ghost appear every time you touch it! Haha!

Anyway, don't mind my dad humor. I hope you enjoy the gift. Think of me when you wear it. Or Anne. Or the summer in London I'm sure you'll never forget!

Much love,
Dad

Malorie couldn't help smiling as she read. Her dad was such a dork, but he was *her* dork, and she couldn't deny that she was happy he had thought of her as he continued his Tudor travels and even thought of sending her a gift!

She clasped the necklace around her throat, admiring the way the golden B glinted in the sunlight. She realized that it was fortunate that her last initial was B, B for Bennington, otherwise folks might question why she was wearing a B around her neck if she had no relevant initial.

She loved the way the fake pearls felt against her skin, cool and smooth, like a soft caress. She realized she adored this necklace and never wanted to take it off. And fortunately, she'd never have to. Anne would live on with her always.

Author's Note

Although elements in this text are true to form, such as many of the facts Peter gave on his tour of the Tower of London and Windsor Castle, as well as the dates of Anne's execution, Elizabeth's birth, and the relative time frame Anne received her letters from Henry, this is ultimately a work of fiction and should be treated as such. I have provided the resources I used in the bibliography that follows.

BIBLIOGRAPHY

Abernethy, Susan. "Where Is King Henry VIII Buried and Why Doesn't He Have a Tomb?" *The Freelance History Writer*, 16 Feb. 2020, https://thefreelancehistorywriter.com/2016/07/29/where-is-king-henry-viii-buried-and-why-doesnt-he-have-a-tomb/.

Barbara, and Barbara. "The Lantern Lobby at Windsor Castle." *The Enchanted Manor*, 14 Apr. 2015, https://theenchantedmanor.com/tag/the-lantern-lobby-at-windsor-castle/#:~:text=Adjacent%20to%20the%20Upper%20Ward,doors%20off%20the%20North%20Terrace.

Berry, Ciara. "Elizabeth I (R.1558-1603)." *The Royal Family*, 3 Aug. 2018, https://www.royal.uk/elizabeth-i#:~:text=Elizabeth%20succeeded%20to%20the%20throne,most%20glorious%20in%20English%20history.

British Library, https://www.bl.uk/collection-items/henry-vlll-songbook.

Claire. "Anne Boleyn's Ladies-in-Waiting." *The Anne Boleyn Files*, 1 Feb. 2013, https://www.theanneboleynfiles.com/anne-boleyns-ladies-in-waiting/.

Claire. "The Vatican Love Letters of Henry VIII - Linda Holds Them!" *The Anne Boleyn Files*, 3 Feb. 2012, https://www.theanneboleynfiles.com/the-vatican-love-letters-of-henry-viii-linda-holds-them/.

"Could Henry VIII Have Had Kell Positive Blood?" *The Tech Interactive*, 12 Feb. 2022, https://www.thetech.org/ask-a-geneticist/henry-viii-kell-blood-type.

"Edward VI." *Encyclopædia Britannica*, Encyclopædia Britannica, Inc., https://www.britannica.com/biography/Edward-VI.

"Explore the Collection." *Royal Collection Trust*, https://www.rct.uk/collection/search#/18/collection/404444/elizabeth-i-when-a-princess.

Explore Three Sides of the Tower's Amazing Story Fortress ... https://www.hrp.org.uk/media/2593/2020-06-29tolmapjune2020.pdf.

Frazza, Brittany. "Anne's Most Telling Piece of Jewelry - Guest Post by Brittany Frazza." *The Anne Boleyn Files*, 3 Oct. 2014, https://www.theanneboleynfiles.com/annes-telling-piece-jewelry-guest-post-brittany-frazza/.

"Henry VIII: The Possessions of a Tudor Monarch." *Medieval Manuscripts Blog*, https://blogs.bl.uk/digitisedmanuscripts/2020/04/henry-viii-the-possessions-of-a-tudor-monarch.html.

Larson, Rebecca. "Love Letters from Henry VIII to Anne Boleyn." *Tudors Dynasty*, 30 July 2016, https://tudorsdynasty.com/love-letter-henry-anne/.

Meares, Hadley. "Why the Last Words of Anne Boleyn Remain a Mystery." *Atlas Obscura*, Atlas Obscura, 14 Apr. 2016, https://www.atlasobscura.com/articles/why-the-last-words-of-anne-boleyn-remain-a-mystery.

"Miniature Whistle Pendant and Anne Boleyn." *On the Tudor Trail*, https://onthetudortrail.com/Blog/2012/01/27/miniature-whistle-pendant-and-anne-boleyn/.

Natalie. "In the Footsteps of Anne Boleyn – the Tower of London." *On the Tudor Trail*, 14 Mar. 2014, https://onthetudortrail.com/Blog/2014/03/02/in-the-footsteps-of-anne-boleyn-the-tower-of-london/#:~:text=On%20the%20morning%20of%2019,one%20of%20his%20admiring%20verses.

pixeltocode.uk, PixelToCode. "Royal Tombs." *Westminster Abbey*, https://www.westminster-abbey.org/about-the-abbey/history/royal-tombs.

Ponti, Crystal. "Who Were the Six Wives of Henry VIII?" *History.com*, A&E Television Networks, 28 Jan. 2020, https://www.history.com/news/henry-viii-wives.

Strawberryhillhouseblog. "Strawberry Hill Spotlights: 'the Clock Still Goes'- Henry VIII's Gift to Anne Boleyn." *Strawberry Hill House Blog*, 9 Oct. 2018, https://strawberryhillhouseblog.wordpress.com/2018/09/10/362/#:~:text=The%20clock%20was%20put%20on,Houses%27%20%27Principal%20Curiosities.

Susan. *Susan Higginbotham*, https://www.susanhigginbotham.com/posts/dressed-to-be-killed-some-tudor-execution-wear/.

Sylwia. "Anne Boleyn – the Glass of Fashion." *Queen Anne Boleyn RSS*, 2 Mar. 2012, http://www.anne-boleyn.com/eng/anne-boleyn-the-glass-of-fashion/.

"The Tower of London - 1000 Long Years as a Royal Palace • the Crown Chronicles." *The Crown Chronicles*, 30 Aug. 2019, https://thecrownchronicles.co.uk/history/history-posts/tower-london-1000-long-years-royal-palace/.

"Traitors' Gate." *Wikipedia*, Wikimedia Foundation, 20 Jan. 2022, https://en.wikipedia.org/wiki/Traitors%27_Gate.

The Tudor Travel Guide, et al. "The Death and Burial of Elizabeth I: Hidden Tales from inside the Vault." *The Tudor Travel Guide*, 20 July 2019, https://thetudortravelguide.com/2019/07/20/the-death-and-burial-of-elizabeth-i/.

The Tudor Travel Guide. "The Royal Apartments at the Tower & the Scandalous Killing of Anne Boleyn." *The Tudor Travel Guide*, The Tudor Travel Guide, 18 Oct. 2021, https://thetudortravelguide.com/2019/05/18/the-royal-apartments-at-the-tower/.

"The White Tower -- Miscellaneous." *Dick and Jane Travel*, https://www.fmschmitt.com/travels/England/london/toweroflondon/firstfloor.html.

"Windsor Castle." *Wikipedia*, Wikimedia Foundation, 27 Mar. 2022, https://en.wikipedia.org/wiki/Windsor_Castle.

ACKNOWLEDGMENTS

I would first like to give thanks to my parents. To my father, Richard, I could not have made it to the finish line without you and I cannot begin to express how much your support, both financial and emotional, has meant to me. To my mother, Lisa, thanks for virtually cheering me on.

To AuthorHouse Publishing, thank you for being willing to take on my work and help a young girl pursue her dream of writing, at least semi-professionally.

To every Anne Boleyn and Tudor Facebook Group I've joined, thank you for sparking the plot of this book and for being a sounding board and fanbase for my work.

To the onthetudortrail blog and many other online resources, which provided me with a lot of useful information. I could not have made this piece half as cohesive without the extensive background information on Henry, Anne, and Elizabeth.

To Shannon Lightcap, thank you for your editing assistance. This story would not have come half as far if you hadn't given me such great insight.

To Emily Chubet, thank you for your graphic design work. It's like you read my mind and created just what I imagined my first book cover to be! You brought the Boleyn necklace to life just as I envisioned it.

To Josh Charette, thank you for helping to edit my book cover. Your AP English teacher should be so proud.

To George, my fur baby and deepest love, even though you will never be able to read this, as you are a dog, I thank you for providing much needed snuggles throughout this journey.

To Zethe King, thanks for giving me the space to write, and thanks for believing in me.

About the Author

Mary Doucette has been an Anne Boleyn fanatic for all of her adult life and is eager to share a twist on Anne's story in her debut novel. Mary graduated from the University of Connecticut with a bachelor's in English and Business Management. She currently lives in Connecticut with her Corgi pup, George. Learn more at www.marys-world.com.